THE TRIMMED LAMP

"Wooed her across the counter with a king cophetua air."

THE
TRIMMED LAMP

AND OTHER STORIES OF
THE FOUR MILLION

BY

O. HENRY, pseud.

*Author of " The Four Million," " The Voice of the
City," " Strictly Business," " Whirligigs,"
" Sixes and Sevens," Etc.*

PUBLISHED BY

DOUBLEDAY, PAGE & COMPANY

FOR

REVIEW OF REVIEWS CO.

1912

CONTENTS

THE TRIMMED LAMP

THE TRIMMED LAMP

OF course there are two sides to the question. Let us look at the other. We often hear " shop-girls " spoken of. No such persons exist. There are girls who work in shops. They make their living that way. But why turn their occupation into an adjective? Let us be fair. We do not refer to the girls who live on Fifth Avenue as " marriage-girls."

Lou and Nancy were chums. They came to the big city to find work because there was not enough to eat at their homes to go around. Nancy was nineteen; Lou was twenty. Both were pretty, active, country girls who had no ambition to go on the stage.

The little cherub that sits up aloft guided them to a cheap and respectable boarding-house. Both found positions and became wage-earners. They remained chums. It is at the end of six months that I would beg you to step forward and be introduced to them. Meddlesome Reader: My Lady friends, Miss Nancy and Miss Lou. While you are shaking hands please take notice — cautiously — of their attire. Yes, cautiously; for they are as quick to resent a stare as a lady in a box at the horse show is.

Lou is a piece-work ironer in a hand laundry. She

[3]

is clothed in a badly-fitting purple dress, and her hat plume is four inches too long; but her ermine muff and scarf cost $25, and its fellow beasts will be ticketed in the windows at $7.98 before the season is over. Her cheeks are pink, and her light blue eyes bright. Contentment radiates from her.

Nancy you would call a shop-girl — because you have the habit. There is no type; but a perverse generation is always seeking a type; so this is what the type should be. She has the high-ratted pompadour, and the exaggerated straight-front. Her skirt is shoddy, but has the correct flare. No furs protect her against the bitter spring air, but she wears her short broadcloth jacket as jauntily as though it were Persian lamb! On her face and in her eyes, remorseless type-seeker, is the typical shop-girl expression. It is a look of silent but contemptuous revolt against cheated womanhood; of sad prophecy of the vengeance to come. When she laughs her loudest the look is still there. The same look can be seen in the eyes of Russian peasants; and those of us left will see it some day on Gabriel's face when he comes to blow us up. It is a look that should wither and abash man; but he has been known to smirk at it and offer flowers — with a string tied to them.

Now lift your hat and come away, while you receive Lou's cheery " See you again," and the sardonic, sweet smile of Nancy that seems, somehow, to miss you and go fluttering like a white moth up over the house-tops to the stars.

The two waited on the corner for Dan. Dan was Lou's steady company. Faithful? Well he was on hand when Mary would have had to hire a dozen sub-poena servers to find her lamb.

" Ain't you cold, Nance? " said Lou. " Say, what a chump you are for working in that old store for $8. a week! I made $18.50 last week. Of course ironing ain't as swell work as selling lace behind a counter, but it pays. None of us ironers make less than $10. And I don't know that it's any less respectful work, either."

" You can have it," said Nancy, with uplifted nose. " I'll take my eight a week and hall bedroom. I like to be among nice things and swell people. And look what a chance I've got! Why, one of our glove girls married a Pittsburg — steel maker, or blacksmith or something — the other day worth a million dollars. I'll catch a swell myself some time. I ain't bragging on my looks or anything; but I'll take my chances where there's big prizes offered. What show would a girl have in a laundry? "

" Why, that's where I met Dan," said Lou, tri-umphantly. " He came in for his Sunday shirt and collars and saw me at the first board, ironing. We all try to get to work at the first board. Ella Magin-nis was sick that day, and I had her place. He said he noticed my arms first, how round and white they was. I had my sleeves rolled up. Some nice fellows come into laundries. You can tell 'em by their bringing their clothes in suit cases, and turning in the door sharp and sudden."

"How can you wear a waist like that, Lou?" said Nancy gazing down at the offending article with sweet scorn in her heavy-lidded eyes. "It shows fierce taste."

"This waist?" cried Lou, with wide-eyed indignation. "Why, I paid $16. for this waist. It's worth twenty-five. A woman left it to be laundered, and never called for it. The boss sold it to me. It's got yards and yards of hand embroidery on it. Better talk about that ugly, plain thing you've got on."

"This ugly, plain thing," said Nancy, calmly, "was copied from one that Mrs. Van Alstyne Fisher was wearing. The girls say her bill in the store last year was $12,000. I made mine, myself. It cost me $1.50. Ten feet away you couldn't tell it from hers."

"Oh, well," said Lou, good-naturedly, "if you want to starve and put on airs, go ahead. But I'll take my job and good wages; and after hours give me something as fancy and attractive to wear as I am able to buy."

But just then Dan came — a serious young man with a ready-made necktie, who had escaped the city's

[6]

brand of frivolity — an electrician earning $30. per week who looked upon Lou with the sad eyes of Romeo, and thought her embroidered waist a web in which any fly should delight to be caught.

" My friend, Mr. Owens — shake hands with Miss Danforth," said Lou.

" I'm mighty glad to know you, Miss Danforth," said Dan, with outstretched hand. " I've heard Lou speak of you so often."

" Thanks," said Nancy, touching his fingers with the tips of her cool ones, " I've heard her mention you — a few times."

Lou giggled.

" Did you get that handshake from Mrs. Van Alstyne Fisher, Nance? " she asked.

" If I did, you can feel safe in copying it," said Nancy.

" Oh, I couldn't use it at all. It's too stylish for me. It's intended to set off diamond rings, that high shake is. Wait till I get a few and then I'll try it."

" Learn it first," said Nancy wisely, " and you'll be more likely to get the rings."

" Now, to settle this argument," said Dan, with his ready, cheerful smile, " let me make a proposition. As I can't take both of you up to Tiffany's and do the right thing, what do you say to a little vaudeville? I've got the tickets. How about looking at stage diamonds since we can't shake hands with the real spark-lers?"

The faithful squire took his place close to the curb; Lou next, a little peacocky in her bright and pretty clothes; Nancy on the inside, slender, and soberly clothed as the sparrow, but with the true Van Alstyne Fisher walk — thus they set out for their evening's moderate diversion.

I do not suppose that many look upon a great department store as an educational institution. But the one in which Nancy worked was something like that to her. She was surrounded by beautiful things that breathed of taste and refinement. If you live in an atmosphere of luxury, luxury is yours whether your money pays for it, or another's.

The people she served were mostly women whose dress, manners, and position in the social world were quoted as criterions. From them Nancy began to take toll — the best from each according to her view.

From one she would copy and practice a gesture, from another an eloquent lifting of an eyebrow, from others, a manner of walking, of carrying a purse, of smiling, of greeting a friend, of addressing " inferiors in station." From her best beloved model, Mrs. Van Alstyne Fisher, she made requisition for that excellent thing, a soft, low voice as clear as silver and as per-fect in articulation as the notes of a thrush. Suffused in the aura of this high social refinement and good breeding, it was impossible for her to escape a deeper effect of it. As good habits are said to be better than good principles, so, perhaps, good manners are better than good habits. The teachings of your parents may not keep alive your New England conscience; but if you sit on a straight-back chair and repeat the words " prisms and pilgrims " forty times the devil will flee from you. And when Nancy spoke in the Van Alstyne Fisher tones she felt the thrill of *noblesse oblige* to her very bones.

There was another source of learning in the great departmental school. Whenever you see three or four shop-girls gather in a bunch and jingle their wire bracelets as an accompaniment to apparently frivolous conversation, do not think that they are there for the purpose of critizing the way Ethel does her back hair. The meeting may lack the dignity of the deliberative bodies of man; but it has all the importance of the occasion on which Eve and her first daughter first put their heads together to make Adam understand his proper place in the household. It is Woman's Conference for Common Defense and Exchange of Strategical Theories of Attack and Repulse upon and against the World, which is a Stage, and Man, its Audience who Persists in Throwing Bouquets Thereupon. Woman, the most helpless of the young of any animal — with the fawn's grace but without its fleetness; with the bird's beauty but without its power

[9]

of flight; with the honey-bee's burden of sweetness but without its — Oh, let's drop that simile — some of us may have been stung.

During this council of war they pass weapons one to another, and exchange stratagems that each has devised and formulated out of the tactics of life.

"I says to 'im," says Sadie, "ain't you the fresh thing! Who do you suppose I am, to be addressing such a remark to me? And what do you think he says back to me?"

The heads, brown, black, flaxen, red, and yellow bob together; the answer is given; and the parry to the thrust is decided upon, to be used by each thereafter in passages-at-arms with the common enemy, man.

Thus Nancy learned the art of defense; and to women successful defense means victory.

The curriculum of a department store is a wide one. Perhaps no other college could have fitted her as well for her life's ambition — the drawing of a matrimonial prize.

Her station in the store was a favored one. The music room was near enough for her to hear and become familiar with the works of the best composers — at least to acquire the familiarity that passed for appreciation in the social world in which she was vaguely trying to set a tentative and aspiring foot. She absorbed the educating influence of art wares, of costly and dainty fabrics, of adornments that are almost culture to women.

The other girls soon became aware of Nancy's ambition. "Here comes your millionaire, Nance," they would call to her whenever any man who looked the rôle approached her counter. It got to be a habit of men, who were hanging about while their women folk were shopping, to stroll over to the handkerchief counter and dawdle over the cambric squares. Nancy's imitation high-bred air and genuine dainty beauty was what attracted. Many men thus came to display their graces before her. Some of them may have been millionaires; others were certainly no more than their sedulous apes. Nancy learned to discriminate. There was a window at the end of the handkerchief counter; and she could see the rows of vehicles waiting for the shoppers in the street below. She looked, and perceived that automobiles differ as well as do their owners.

Once a fascinating gentleman bought four dozen handkerchiefs, and wooed her across the counter with a King Cophetua air. When he had gone one of the girls said:

"What's wrong, Nance, that you didn't warm up to that fellow? He looks the swell article, all right, to me."

"Him?" said Nancy, with her coolest, sweetest, most impersonal, Van Alstyne Fisher smile; "not for

[11]

mine. I saw him drive up outside. A 12 H. P. machine and an Irish chauffeur! And you saw what kind of handkerchiefs he bought — silk! And he's got dactylis on him. Give me the real thing or nothing, if you please."

Two of the most "refined" women in the store — a forelady and a cashier — had a few "swell gentlemen friends" with whom they now and then dined. Once they included Nancy in an invitation. The dinner took place in a spectacular café whose tables are engaged for New Year's eve a year in advance. There were two "gentlemen friends" — one without any hair on his head — high living ungrew it; and we can prove it — the other a young man whose worth and sophistication he impressed upon you in two convincing ways — he swore that all the wine was corked; and he wore diamond cuff bottons. This young man perceived irresistible excellencies in Nancy. His taste ran to shop-girls; and here was one that added the voice and manners of his high social world to the franker charms of her own caste. So, on the following day, he appeared in the store and made her a serious proposal of marriage over a box of hemstitched, grass-bleached Irish linens. Nancy declined. A brown pompadour ten feet away had been using her eyes and ears. When the rejected suitor had gone she heaped carboys of upbraidings and horror upon Nancy's head.

" What a terrible little fool you are! That fellow's

a millionaire — he's a nephew of old Van Skittles himself. And he was talking on the level, too. Have you gone crazy, Nance?"

"Have I?" said Nancy. "I didn't take him, did I? He isn't a millionaire so hard that you could notice it, anyhow. His family only allows him $20,000 a year to spend. The bald-headed fellow was guying him about it the other night at supper."

The brown pompadour came nearer and narrowed her eyes.

"Say, what do you want?" she inquired, in a voice hoarse for lack of chewing-gum. "Ain't that enough for you? Do you want to be a Mormon, and marry Rockefeller and Gladstone Dowie and the King of Spain and the whole bunch? Ain't $20,000 a year good enough for you?"

Nancy flushed a little under the level gaze of the black, shallow eyes.

"It wasn't altogether the money, Carrie," she explained. "His friend caught him in a rank lie the other night at dinner. It was about some girl he said he hadn't been to the theater with. Well, I can't stand a liar. Put everything together — I don't like him; and that settles it. When I sell out it's not going to be on any bargain day. I've got to have something that sits up in a chair like a man, anyhow. Yes, I'm looking out for a catch; but it's got to be able to do something more than make a noise like a toy bank."

[13]

" The physiopathic ward for yours!" said the brown pompadour, walking away.

These high ideas, if not ideals — Nancy continued to cultivate on $8. per week. She bivouacked on the trail of the great unknown " catch," eating her dry bread and tightening her belt day by day. On her face was the faint, soldierly, sweet, grim smile of the preordained man-hunter. The store was her forest; and many times she raised her rifle at game that seemed broad-antlered and big; but always some deep unerring instinct — perhaps of the huntress, perhaps of the woman — made her hold her fire and take up the trail again.

Lou flourished in the laundry. Out of her $18.50 per week she paid $6. for her room and board. The rest went mainly for clothes. Her opportunities for bettering her taste and manners were few compared with Nancy's. In the steaming laundry there was nothing but work, work and her thoughts of the evening pleasures to come. Many costly and showy fabrics passed under her iron; and it may be that her growing fondness for dress was thus transmitted to her through the conducting metal.

When the day's work was over Dan awaited her outside, her faithful shadow in whatever light she stood.

Sometimes he cast an honest and troubled glance at Lou's clothes that increased in conspicuity rather than in style; but this was no disloyalty; he deprecated the attention they called to her in the streets.

And Lou was no less faithful to her chum. There was a law that Nancy should go with them on whatsoever outings they might take. Dan bore the extra burden heartily and in good cheer. It might be said that Lou furnished the color, Nancy the tone, and Dan the weight of the distraction-seeking trio. The escort, in his neat but obviously ready-made suit, his ready-made tie and unfailing, genial, ready-made wit never startled or clashed. He was of that good kind that you are likely to forget while they are present, but remember distinctly after they are gone.

To Nancy's superior taste the flavor of these ready-made pleasures was sometimes a little bitter: but she was young; and youth is a gourmand, when it cannot be a gourmet.

"Dan is always wanting me to marry him right away," Lou told her once. "But why should I. I'm independent. I can do as I please with the money I earn; and he never would agree for me to keep on working afterward. And say, Nance, what do you want to stick to that old store for, and half starve and half dress yourself? I could get you a place in the laundry right now if you'd come. It seems to me that you could afford to be a little less stuck-up if you could make a good deal more money."

"I don't think I'm stuck-up, Lou," said Nancy,

[15]

" but I'd rather live on half rations and stay where I am. I suppose I've got the habit. It's the chance that I want. I don't expect to be always behind a counter. I'm learning something new every day. I'm right up against refined and rich people all the time — even if I do only wait on them; and I'm not missing any pointers that I see passing around."

" Caught your millionaire yet? " asked Lou with her teasing laugh.

" I haven't selected one yet," answered Nancy. " I've been looking them over."

" Goodness! the idea of picking over 'em! Don't you ever let one get by you Nance — even if he's a few dollars shy. But of course you're joking — millionaires don't think about working girls like us."

" It might be better for them if they did," said Nancy, with cool wisdom. " Some of us could teach them how to take care of their money."

" If one was to speak to me," laughed Lou, " I know I'd have a duck-fit."

" That's because you don't know any. The only difference between swells and other people is you have to watch 'em closer. Don't you think that red silk lining is just a little bit too bright for that coat, Lou? "

Lou looked at the plain, dull olive jacket of her friend.

" Well, no I don't — but it may seem so beside that faded-looking thing you've got on."

" This jacket," said Nancy, complacently, " has exactly the cut and fit of one that Mrs. Van Alstyne Fisher was wearing the other day. The material cost me $3.98. I suppose hers cost about $100. more."

" Oh, well," said Lou lightly, " it don't strike me as millionaire bait. Shouldn't wonder if I catch one before you do, anyway."

Truly it would have taken a philosopher to decide upon the values of the theories held by the two friends. Lou, lacking that certain pride and fastidiousness that keeps stores and desks filled with girls working for the barest living, thumped away gaily with her iron in the noisy and stifling laundry. Her wages supported her even beyond the point of comfort; so that her dress profited until sometimes she cast a sidelong glance of impatience at the neat but inelegant apparel of Dan — Dan the constant, the immutable, the undeviating.

As for Nancy, her case was one of tens of thousands. Silk and jewels and laces and ornaments and the perfume and music of the fine world of good-breeding and taste — these were made for woman; they are her equitable portion. Let her keep near them if they are a part of life to her, and if she will. She is no traitor to herself, as Esau was; for she keeps her birthright and the pottage she earns is often very scant.

In this atmosphere Nancy belonged; and she throve

[17]

in it and ate her frugal meals and schemed over her cheap dresses with a determined and contented mind. She already knew woman; and she was studying man, the animal, both as to his habits and eligibility. Some day she would bring down the game that she wanted; but she promised herself it would be what seemed to her the biggest and the best, and nothing smaller.

Thus she kept her lamp trimmed and burning to receive the bridegroom when he should come.

But, another lesson she learned, perhaps unconsciously. Her standard of values began to shift and change. Sometimes the dollar-mark grew blurred in her mind's eye, and shaped itself into letters that spelled such words as " truth " and " honor " and now and then just " kindness." Let us make a likeness of one who hunts the moose or elk in some mighty wood. He sees a little dell, mossy and embowered, where a rill trickles, babbling to him of rest and comfort. At these times the spear of Nimrod himself grows blunt.

So, Nancy wondered sometimes if Persian lamb was always quoted at its market value by the hearts that it covered.

One Thursday evening Nancy left the store and turned across Sixth Avenue westward to the laundry. She was expected to go with Lou and Dan to a musical comedy.

Dan was just coming out of the laundry when she

arrived. There was a queer, strained look on his face.

"I thought I would drop around to see if they had heard from her," he said.

"Heard from who?" asked Nancy. "Isn't Lou there?"

"I thought you knew," said Dan. "She hasn't been here or at the house where she lived since Monday. She moved all her things from there. She told one of the girls in the laundry she might be going to Europe."

"Hasn't anybody seen her anywhere?" asked Nancy.

Dan looked at her with his jaws set grimly, and a steely gleam in his steady gray eyes.

"They told me in the laundry," he said, harshly, "that they saw her pass yesterday — in an automobile. With one of the millionaires, I suppose, that you and Lou were forever busying your brains about."

For the first time Nancy quailed before a man. She laid her hand that trembled slightly on Dan's sleeve.

"You've no right to say such a thing to me Dan — as if I had anything to do with it!"

"I didn't mean it that way," said Dan, softening. He fumbled in his vest pocket.

"I've got the tickets for the show to-night," he said, with a gallant show of lightness. "If you —"

Nancy admired pluck whenever she saw it.

[19]

" I'll go with you, Dan," she said.

Three months went by before Nancy saw Lou again.

At twilight one evening the shop-girl was hurrying home along the border of a little quiet park. She heard her name called, and wheeled about in time to catch Lou rushing into her arms.

After the first embrace they drew their heads back as serpents do, ready to attack or to charm, with a thousand questions trembling on their swift tongues. And then Nancy noticed that prosperity had descended upon Lou, manifesting itself in costly furs, flashing gems, and creations of the tailors' art.

" You little fool! " cried Lou, loudly and affectionately. " I see you are still working in that store, and as shabby as ever. And how about that big catch you were going to make — nothing doing yet, I suppose? "

And then Lou looked, and saw that something better than prosperity had descended upon Nancy — something that shone brighter than gems in her eyes and redder than a rose in her cheeks, and that danced like electricity, anxious to be loosed from the tip of her tongue.

" Yes, I'm still in the store," said Nancy, " but I'm going to leave it next week. I've made my catch — the biggest catch in the world. You won't mind now Lou, will you? — I'm going to be married to Dan — to Dan! — he's my Dan now — why, Lou! "

Around the corner of the park strolled one of those
new-crop, smooth-faced young policemen that are making the force more endurable — at least to the eye.
He saw a woman with an expensive fur coat and dia-
mond-ringed hands crouching down against the iron
fence of the park sobbing turbulently, while a slender,
plainly-dressed working girl leaned close, trying to
console her. But the Gibsonian cop, being of the new
order, passed on, pretending not to notice, for he was
wise enough to know that these matters are beyond
help, so far as the power he represents is concerned,
though he rap the pavement with his nightstick till the
sound goes up to the furthermost stars.

A MADISON SQUARE ARABIAN NIGHT

TO Carson Chalmers, in his apartment near the square, Phillips brought the evening mail. Besides the routine correspondence there were two items bearing the same foreign postmark.

One of the incoming parcels contained a photograph of a woman. The other contained an interminable letter, over which Chalmers hung, absorbed, for a long time. The letter was from another woman; and it contained poisoned barbs, sweetly dipped in honey, and feathered with innuendoes concerning the photographed woman.

Chalmers tore this letter into a thousand bits and began to wear out his expensive rug by striding back and forth upon it. Thus an animal from the jungle acts when it is caged, and thus a caged man acts when he is housed in a jungle of doubt.

By and by the restless mood was overcome. The rug was not an enchanted one. For sixteen feet he could travel along it; three thousand miles was beyond its power to aid.

Phillips appeared. He never entered; he invariably appeared, like a well-oiled genie.

"Will you dine here, sir, or out?" he asked.

A MADISON SQUARE ARABIAN NIGHT

"Here," said Chalmers, "and in half an hour." He listened glumly to the January blasts making an Aeolian trombone of the empty street.

"Wait," he said to the disappearing genie. "As I came home across the end of the square I saw many men standing there in rows. There was one mounted upon something, talking. Why do those men stand in rows, and why are they there?"

"They are homeless men, sir," said Phillips. "The man standing on the box tries to get lodging for them for the night. People come around to listen and give him money. Then he sends as many as the money will pay for to some lodging-house. That is why they stand in rows; they get sent to bed in order as they come."

"By the time dinner is served," said Chalmers, "have one of those men here. He will dine with me."

"W-w-which —," began Phillips, stammering for the first time during his service.

"Choose one at random," said Chalmers. "You might see that he is reasonably sober — and a certain amount of cleanliness will not be held against him. That is all."

It was an unusual thing for Carson Chalmers to play the Caliph. But on that night he felt the inefficacy of conventional antidotes to melancholy. Something wanton and egregious, something high-flavored and Arabian, he must have to lighten his mood.

On the half hour Phillips had finished his duties as slave of the lamp. The waiters from the restaurant below had whisked aloft the delectable dinner. The dining table, laid for two, glowed cheerily in the glow of the pink-shaded candles.

And now Phillips, as though he ushered a cardinal — or held in charge a burglar — wafted in the shivering guest who had been haled from the line of mendicant lodgers.

It is a common thing to call such men wrecks; if the comparison be used here it is the specific one of a derelict come to grief through fire. Even yet some flickering combustion illuminated the drifting hulk. His face and hands had been recently washed — a rite insisted upon by Phillips as a memorial to the slaughtered conventions. In the candle-light he stood, a flaw in the decorous fittings of the apartment. His face was a sickly white, covered almost to the eyes with a stubble the shade of a red Irish setter's coat. Phillips's comb had failed to control the pale brown hair, long matted and conformed to the contour of a constantly worn hat. His eyes were full of a hopeless, tricky defiance like that seen in a cur's that is cornered by his tormentors. His shabby coat was buttoned high, but a quarter inch of redeeming collar showed above it. His manner was singularly free from embarrassment when Chalmers rose from his chair across the round dining table.

" If you will oblige me," said the host, " I will be glad to have your company at dinner."

" My name is Plumer," said the highway guest, in harsh and aggressive tones. " If you're like me, you like to know the name of the party you're dining with."

" I was going on to say," continued Chalmers some-what hastily, " that mine is Chalmers. Will you sit opposite? "

Plumer, of the ruffled plumes, bent his knees for Phillips to slide the chair beneath him. He had an air of having sat at attended boards before. Phillips set out the anchovies and olives.

" Good! " barked Plumer; " Going to be in courses, it it? All right, my jovial ruler of Bagdad. I'm your Scheherezade all the way to the toothpicks. You're the first Caliph with a genuine Oriental flavor I've struck since frost. What luck! And I was forty-third in line. I finished counting just as your welcome emissary arrived to bid me to the feast. I had about as much chance of getting a bed to-night as I have of being the next President. How will you have the sad story of my life, Mr. Al Raschid — a chapter with each course or the whole edition with the cigars and coffee? "

"The situation does not seem a novel one to you," said Chalmers with a smile.

"By the chin whiskers of the prophet — no!" answered the guest. "New York's as full of cheap Haroun al Raschids as Bagdad is of fleas. I've been held up for my story with a loaded meal pointed at my head twenty times. Catch anybody in New York giving you something for nothing! They spell curiosity and charity with the same set of building blocks. Lots of 'em will stake you to a dime and chop-suey; and a few of 'em will play Caliph to the tune of a top sirloin; but every one of 'em will stand over you till they screw your autobiography out of you with foot notes, appendix and unpublished fragments. Oh, I know what to do when I see victuals coming toward me in little old Bagdad-on-the-Subway. I strike the asphalt three times with my forehead and get ready to spiel yarns for my supper. I claim descent from the late Tommy Tucker, who was forced to hand out vocal harmony for his pre-digested wheaterina and spoopju."

"I do not ask your story," said Chalmers. "I tell you frankly that it was a sudden whim that prompted me to send for some stranger to dine with me. I assure you you will not suffer through any curiosity of mine."

"Oh, fudge!" exclaimed the guest, enthusiastically tackling his soup; "I don't mind it a bit. I'm a reg'

ular Oriental magazine with a red cover and the leaves cut when the Caliph walks abroad. In fact, we fellows in the bed line have a sort of union rate for things of this sort. Somebody's always stopping and wanting to know what brought us down so low in the world. For a sandwich and a glass of beer I tell 'em that drink did it. For corned beef and cabbage and a cup of coffee I give 'em the hard-hearted-landlord — six-months-in-the-hospital-lost-job story. A sirloin steak and a quarter for a bed gets the Wall Street tragedy of the swept-away fortune and the gradual descent. This is the first spread of this kind I've stumbled against. I haven't got a story to fit it. I'll tell you what, Mr. Chalmers, I'm going to tell you the truth for this, if you'll listen to it. It'll be harder for you to believe than the made-up ones."

An hour later the Arabian guest lay back with a sigh of satisfaction while Phillips brought the coffee and cigars and cleared the table.

" Did you ever hear of Sherrard Plumer? " he asked, with a strange smile.

" I remember the name," said Chalmers. " He was a painter, I think, of a good deal of prominence a few years ago."

" Five years," said the guest. " Then I went down like a chunk of lead. I'm Sherrard Plumer! I sold the last portrait I painted for $2,000. After that I couldn't have found a sitter for a gratis picture "

"What was the trouble?" Chalmers could not resist asking.

"Funny thing," answered Plumer, grimly. "Never quite understood it myself. For a while I swam like a cork. I broke into the swell crowd and got commissions right and left. The newspapers called me a fashionable painter. Then the funny things began to happen. Whenever I finished a picture people would come to see it, and whisper and look queerly at one another.

"I soon found out what the trouble was. I had a knack of bringing out in the face of a portrait the hidden character of the original. I don't know how I did it — I painted what I saw — but I know it did me. Some of my sitters were fearfully enraged and refused their pictures. I painted the portrait of a very beautiful and popular society dame. When it was finished her husband looked at it with a peculiar expression on his face, and the next week he sued for divorce.

"I remember one case of a prominent banker who sat to me. While I had his portrait on exhibition in my studio an acquaintance of his came in to look at it. 'Bless me,' says he, 'does he really look like that?' I told him it was considered a faithful likeness. 'I never noticed that expression about his eyes before,' said he; 'I think I'll drop downtown and change my bank account.' He did drop down, but

[28]

the bank account was gone and so was Mr. Banker.

"It wasn't long till they put me out of business. People don't want their secret meannesses shown up in a picture. They can smile and twist their own faces and deceive you, but the picture can't. I couldn't get an order for another picture, and I had to give up. I worked as a newspaper artist for a while, and then for a lithographer, but my work with them got me into the same trouble. If I drew from a photograph my drawing showed up characteristics and expressions that you couldn't find in the photo, but I guess they were in the original, all right. The customers raised lively rows, especially the women, and I never could hold a job long. So I began to rest my weary head upon the breast of Old Booze for comfort. And pretty soon I was in the free-bed line and doing oral fiction for hand-outs among the food bazaars. Does the truthful statement weary thee, O Caliph? I can turn on the Wall Street disaster stop if you prefer, but that requires a tear, and I'm afraid I can't hustle one up after that good dinner."

"No, no," said Chalmers, earnestly, "you interest me very much. Did all of your portraits reveal some unpleasant trait, or were there some that did not suffer from the ordeal of your peculiar brush?"

"Some? Yes," said Plumer. "Children generally, a good many women and a sufficient number of men. All people aren't bad, you know. When they, were all right the pictures were all right. As I said, I don't explain it, but I'm telling you facts."

On Chalmer's writing-table lay the photograph that he had received that day in the foreign mail. Ten minutes later he had Plumber at work making a sketch from it in pastels. At the end of an hour the artist rose and stretched wearily.

"It's done," he yawned. "You'll excuse me for being so long. I got interested in the job. Lordy! but I'm tired. No bed last night, you know. Guess it'll have to be good night now, O Commander of the Faithful!"

Chalmers went as far as the door with him and slipped some bills into his hand.

"Oh! I'll take 'em," said Plumer. "All that's included in the fall. Thanks. And for the very good dinner. I shall sleep on feathers to-night and dream of Bagdad. I hope it won't turn out to be a dream in the morning. Farewell, most excellent Caliph!"

Again Chalmers paced restlessly upon his rug. But his beat lay as far from the table whereon lay the pastel sketch as the room would permit. Twice, thrice, he tried to approach it, but failed. He could see the dun and gold and brown of the colors, but there was a wall about it built by his fears that kept him at a distance. He sat down and tried to calm himself. He sprang up and rang for Phillips.

"There is a young artist in this building," he said,

"— a Mr. Reineman — do you know which is his apartment?"

"Top floor, front, sir," said Phillips.

"Go up and ask him to favor me with his presence here for a few minutes."

Reineman came at once. Chalmers introduced himself.

"Mr. Reineman," said he, "there is a little pastel sketch on yonder table. I would be glad if you will give me your opinion of it as to its artistic merits and as a picture."

The young artist advanced to the table and took up the sketch. Chalmers half turned away, leaning upon the back of a chair.

"How — do — you — find it?" he asked, slowly.

"As a drawing," said the artist, "I can't praise it enough. It's the work of a master — bold and fine and true. It puzzles me a little; I haven't seen any pastel work near as good in years."

"The face, man — the subject — the original — what would you say of that?"

"The face," said Reineman, "is the face of one of God's own angels. May I ask who —"

"My wife!" shouted Chalmers, wheeling and pouncing upon the astonished artist, gripping his hand and pounding his back. "She is traveling in Europe. Take that sketch, boy, and paint the picture of your life from it and leave the price to me."

THE RUBAIYAT OF A SCOTCH HIGHBALL

THIS document is intended to strike somewhere between a temperance lecture and the "Bartender's
Guide." Relative to the latter, drink shall swell the
theme and be set forth in abundance. Agreeably to
the former, not an elbow shall be crooked.

Bob Babbitt was "off the stuff." Which means —
as you will discover by referring to the unabridged
dictionary of Bohemia — that he had "cut out the
booze;" that he was "on the water wagon." The
reason for Bob's sudden attitude of hostility toward
the "demon rum"— as the white ribboners miscall
whiskey (see the "Bartender's Guide"), should be
of interest to reformers and saloon-keepers.

There is always hope for a man who, when sober,
will not concede or acknowledge that he was ever drunk.
But when a man will say (in the apt words of the
phrase-distiller), "I had a beautiful skate on last
night," you will have to put stuff in his coffee as well
as pray for him.

One evening on his way home Babbitt dropped in at
the Broadway bar that he liked best. Always there
were three or four fellows there from the downtown
offices whom he knew. And then there would be high-

[32]

balls and stories, and he would hurry home to dinner
a little late but feeling good, and a little sorry for the
poor Standard Oil Company. On this evening as he
entered he heard some one say: " Babbitt was in last
night as full as a boiled owl."

Babbitt walked to the bar, and saw in the mirror
that his face was as white as chalk. For the first time
he had looked Truth in the eyes. Others had lied to
him; he had dissembled with himself. He was a
drunkard, and had not known it. What he had
fondly imagined was a pleasant exhilaration had been
maudlin intoxication. His fancied wit had been
drivel; his gay humors nothing but the noisy vagaries
of a sot. But, never again!

" A glass of seltzer," he said to the bartender.

A little silence fell upon the group of his cronies,
who had been expecting him to join them.

" Going off the stuff, Bob? " one of them asked
politely and with more formality than the highballs
ever called forth.

" Yes," said Babbitt.

Some one of the group took up the unwashed thread
of a story he had been telling; the bartender shoved
over a dime and a nickel change from the quarter, un-
garnished with his customary smile; and Babbitt
walked out.

Now, Babbitt had a home and a wife — but that is
another story. And I will tell you that story, which

will show you a better habit and a worse story than
you could find in the man who invented the phrase.

It began away up in Sullivan County, where so
many rivers and so much trouble begins — or begin;
how would you say that? It was July, and Jessie was
a summer boarder at the Mountain Squint Hotel, and
Bob, who was just out of college, saw her one day —
and they were married in September. That's the
tabloid novel — one swallow of water, and it's gone.

But those July days!

Let the exclamation point expound it, for I shall
not. For particulars you might read up on " Romeo
and Juliet," and Abraham Lincoln's thrilling sonnet
about " You can fool some of the people," &c., and
Darwin's works.

But one thing I must tell you about. Both of them
were mad over Omar's Rubaiyat. They knew every
verse of the old bluffer by heart — not consecutively,
but picking 'em out here and there as you fork the
mushrooms in a fifty-cent steak á la Bordelaise. Sullivan County is full of rocks and trees; and Jessie used
to sit on them, and — please be good — used to sit on
the rocks; and Bob had a way of standing behind her
with his hands over her shoulders holding her hands,
and his face close to hers, and they would repeat over
and over their favorite verses of the old tent-maker.
They saw only the poetry and philosophy of the lines
then — indeed, they agreed that the Wine was only

an image, and that what was meant to be celebrated was some divinity, or maybe Love or Life. However, at that time neither of them had tasted the stuff that goes with a sixty-cent *table d'hote*.

Where was I? Oh, they married and came to New York. Bob showed his college diploma, and accepted a position filling inkstands in a lawyer's office at $15 a week. At the end of two years he had worked up to $50, and gotten his first taste of Bohemia — the kind that won't stand the borax and formaldehyde tests.

They had two furnished rooms and a little kitchen. To Jess, accustomed to the mild but beautiful savor of a country town, the dreggy Bohemia was sugar and spice. She hung fish seines on the walls of her rooms, and bought a rakish-looking sideboard, and learned to play the banjo. Twice or thrice a week they dined at French or Italian *tables d'hote* in a cloud of smoke, and brag and unshorn hair. Jess learned to drink a cocktail in order to get the cherry. At home she smoked a cigarette after dinner. She learned to pronounce Chianti, and leave her olive stones for the waiter to pick up. Once she essayed to say la, la, la! in a crowd; but got only as far as the second one. They met one or two couples while dining out and became friendly with them. The sideboard was stocked with Scotch and rye and a liqueur. They had their new friends in to dinner and all were laughing at nothing by 1 A. M. Some plastering fell in the

room below them, for which Bob had to pay $4.50.
Thus they footed it merrily on the ragged frontiers of
the country that has no boundary lines or government.

And soon Bob fell in with his cronies and learned
to keep his foot on the little rail six inches above the
floor for an hour or so every afternoon before he
went home. Drink always rubbed him the right way,
and he would reach his rooms as jolly as a sandboy.
Jessie would meet him at the door, and generally they
would dance some insane kind of a rigadoon about the
floor by way of greeting. Once when Bob's feet became confused and he tumbled headlong over a foot-
stool Jessie laughed so heartily and long that he had to
throw all the couch pillows at her to make her hush.

In such wise life was speeding for them on the day
when Bob Babbitt first felt the power that the giftie
gi'ed him.

But let us get back to our lamb and mint sauce.

When Bob got home that evening he found Jessie
in a long apron cutting up a lobster for the Newburg.
Usually when Bob came in mellow from his hour at the
bar his welcome was hilarious, though somewhat tinc-
tured with Scotch smoke.

By screams and snatches of song and certain audible
testimonials to domestic felicity was his advent proclaimed. When she heard his foot on the stairs the
old maid in the hall room always stuffed cotton into
her ears. At first Jessie had shrunk from the rude-

ness and flavor of these spiritual greetings, but as the fog of the false Bohemia gradually encompassed her she came to accept them as love's true and proper greeting.

Bob came in without a word, smiled, kissed her neatly but noiselessly, took up a paper and sat down. In the hall room the old maid held her two plugs of cotton poised, filled with anxiety.

Jessie dropped lobster and knife and ran to him with frightened eyes.

" What's the matter, Bob, are you ill? "

" Not at all, dear."

" Then what's the matter with you? "

" Nothing."

Hearken, brethren. When She-who-has-a-right-to-ask interrogates you concerning a change she finds in your mood answer her thus: Tell her that you, in a sudden rage, have murdered your grandmother; tell her that you have robbed orphans and that remorse has stricken you; tell her your fortune is swept away; that you are beset by enemies, by bunions, by any kind of malevolent fate; but do not, if peace and happiness are worth as much as a grain of mustard seed to you — do not answer her " Nothing."

Jessie went back to the lobster in silence. She cast looks of darkest suspicion at Bob. He had never acted that way before.

When dinner was on the table she set out the bottle of Scotch and the glasses. Bob declined.

" Tell you the truth, Jess," he said. " I've cut out the drink. Help yourself, of course. If you don't mind I'll try some of the seltzer straight."

" You've stopped drinking? " she said, looking at him steadily and unsmilingly. " What for? "

" It wasn't doing me any good," said Bob. " Don't you approve of the idea? "

Jessie raised her eyebrows and one shoulder slightly.

" Entirely," she said with a sculptured smile. " I could not conscientiously advise any one to drink or smoke, or whistle on Sunday."

The meal was finished almost in silence. Bob tried to make talk, but his efforts lacked the stimulus of previous evenings. He felt miserable, and once or twice his eye wandered toward the bottle, but each time the scathing words of his bibulous friend sounded in his ear, and his mouth set with determination.

Jessie felt the change deeply. The essence of their lives seemed to have departed suddenly. The restless fever, the false gayety, the unnatural excitement of the shoddy Bohemia in which they had lived had dropped away in the space of the popping of a cork. She stole curious and forlorn glances at the dejected Bob, who bore the guilty look of at least a wife-beater or a family tyrant.

After dinner the colored maid who came in daily

[38]

to perform such chores cleared away the things. Jessie, with as unreadable countenance, brought back the bottle of Scotch and the glasses and a bowl of cracked ice and set them on the table.

"May I ask," she said, with some of the ice in her tones, "whether I am to be included in your sudden spasm of goodness? If not, I'll make one for myself. It's rather chilly this evening, for some reason."

"Oh, come now, Jess," said Bob good-naturedly, "don't be too rough on me. Help yourself, by all means. There's no danger of your overdoing it. But I thought there was with me; and that's why I quit. Have yours, and then let's get out the banjo and try over that new quickstep."

"I've heard," said Jessie in the tones of the oracle, "that drinking alone is a pernicious habit. No, I don't think I feel like playing this evening. If we are going to reform we may as well abandon the evil habit of banjo-playing, too."

She took up a book and sat in her little willow rocker on the other side of the table. Neither of them spoke for half an hour.

And then Bob laid down his paper and got up with a strange, absent look on his face and went behind her chair and reached over her shoulders, taking her hands in his, and laid his face close to hers.

In a moment to Jessie the walls of the seine-hung room vanished, and she saw the Sullivan County hills

[39]

and rills. Bob felt her hands quiver in his as he began the verse from old Omar:

> " Come, fill the Cup, and in the Fire of Spring
>   The Winter Garment of Repentance fling:
>   The Bird of Time has but a little way
>   To fly — and Lo! the Bird is on the Wing! "

And then he walked to the table and poured a stiff drink of Scotch into a glass.

But in that moment a mountain breeze had somehow found its way in and blown away the mist of the false Bohemia.

Jessie leaped and with one fierce sweep of her hand sent the bottle and glasses crashing to the floor. The same motion of her arm carried it around Bob's neck, where it met its mate and fastened tight.

" Oh, my God, Bobbie — not that verse — I see now. I wasn't always such a fool, was I? The other one, boy — the one that says: ' Remould it to the Heart's Desire.' Say that one —' to the Heart's Desire.' "

" I know that one," said Bob. " It goes:

> " ' Ah! Love, could you and I with Him conspire
>   To grasp this sorry Scheme of Things entire
>   Would not we—' "

" Let me finish it," said Jessie.

> " ' Would not we shatter it to bits — and then
>   Remould it nearer to the Heart's Desire! ' "

[40]

"It's shattered all right," said Bob, crunching some glass under his heel.

In some dungeon below the accurate ear of Mrs. Pickens, the landlady, located the smash.

"It's that wild Mr. Babbitt coming home soused again," she said. "And he's got such a nice little wife, too!"

THE PENDULUM

"EIGHTY-FIRST Street — let 'em out, please,"
yelled the shepherd in blue.

A flock of citizen sheep scrambled out and another
flock scrambled aboard. Ding-ding! The cattle cars
of the Manhattan Elevated rattled away, and John
Perkins drifted down the stairway of the station with
the released flock.

John walked slowly toward his flat. Slowly, because in the lexicon of his daily life there was no such
word as " perhaps." There are no surprises awaiting
a man who has been married two years and lives in a
flat. As he walked John Perkins prophesied to himself with gloomy and downtrodden cynicism the fore-
gone conclusions of the monotonous day.

Katy would meet him at the door with a kiss flavored with cold cream and butter-scotch. He would
remove his coat, sit upon a macadamized lounge and
read, in the evening paper, of Russians and Japs
slaughtered by the deadly linotype. For dinner there
would be pot roast, a salad flavored with a dressing
warranted not to crack or injure the leather, stewed
rhubarb and the bottle of strawberry marmalade blushing at the certificate of chemical purity on its label.

After dinner Katy would show him the new patch in her crazy quilt that the iceman had cut for her off the end of his four-in-hand. At half-past seven they would spread newspapers over the furniture to catch the pieces of plastering that fell when the fat man in the flat overhead began to take his physical culture exercises. Exactly at eight \Hickey & Mooney, of the vaudeville team (unbooked) in the flat across the hall, would yield to the gentle influence of delirium tremens and begin to overturn chairs under the delusion that Hammerstein was pursuing them with a five-hundred-dollar-a-week contract. Then the gent at the window across the air-shaft would get out his flute; the nightly gas leak would steal forth to frolic in the highways; the dumbwaiter would slip off its trolley; the janitor would drive Mrs. Zanowitski's five children once more across the Yalu, the lady with the champagne shoes and the Skye terrier would trip downstairs and paste her Thursday name over her bell and letter-box — and the evening routine of the Frogmore flats would be under way.

John Perkins knew these things would happen. And he knew that at a quarter past eight he would summon his nerve and reach for his hat, and that his wife would deliver this speech in a querulous tone:

" Now, where are you going, I'd like to know, John Perkins? "

" Thought I'd drop up to McCloskey's," he would

answer, " and play a game or two of pool with the fellows."

Of late such had been John Perkin's habit. At ten or eleven he would return. Sometimes Katy would be asleep; sometimes waiting up, ready to melt in the crucible of her ire a little more gold plating from the wrought steel chains of matrimony. For these things Cupid will have to answer when he stands at the bar of justice with his victims from the Frogmore flats.

To-night John Perkins encountered a tremendous upheaval of the commonplace when he reached his door. No Katy was there with her affectionate, confectionate kiss. The three rooms seemed in portentous disorder. All about lay her things in confusion. Shoes in the middle of the floor, curling tongs, hair bows, kimonos, powder box, jumbled together on dresser and chairs — this was not Katy's way. With a sinking heart John saw the comb with a curling cloud of her brown hair among its teeth. Some unusual hurry and perturbation must have possessed her, for she always carefully placed these combings in the little blue vase on the mantel to be some day formed into the coveted feminine " rat."

Hanging conspicuously to the gas jet by a string was a folded paper. John seized it. It was a note from his wife running thus:

THE PENDULUM

*" Dear John: I just had a telegram saying mother
is very sick. I am going to take the 4.30 train.
Brother Sam is going to meet me at the depot there.
There is cold mutton in the ice box. I hope it isn't
her quinzy again. Pay the milkman 60 cents. She
had it bad last spring. Don't forget to write to the
company about the gas meter, and your good socks
are in the top drawer. I will write to-morrow.*
Hastily,   KATY."

Never during their two years of matrimony had
he and Katy been separated for a night. John read
the note over and over in a dumfounded way. Here
was a break in a routine that had never varied, and
it left him dazed.

There on the back of a chair hung, pathetically
empty and formless, the red wrapper with black dots
that she always wore while getting the meals. Her
week-day clothes had been tossed here and there in
her haste. A little paper bag of her favorite butter-
scotch lay with its string yet unwound. A daily
paper sprawled on the floor, gaping rectangularly
where a railroad time-table had been clipped from it.
Everything in the room spoke of a loss, of an essence
gone, of its soul and life departed. John Perkins
stood among the dead remains with a queer feeling of
desolation in his heart.

He began to set the rooms tidy as well as he could.

[45]

When he touched her clothes a thrill of something like terror went through him. He had never thought what existence would be without Katy. She had become so thoroughly annealed into his life that she was like the air he breathed — necessary but scarcely noticed. Now, without warning, she was gone, vanished, as completely absent as if she had never existed. Of course it would be only for a few days, or at most a week or two, but it seemed to him as if the very hand of death had pointed a finger at his secure and un-eventful home.

John dragged the cold mutton from the ice-box, made coffee and sat down to a lonely meal face to face with the strawberry marmalade's shameless certificate of purity. Bright among withdrawn blessings now appeared to him the ghosts of pot roast and the salad with tan polish dressing. His home was dismantled. A quinzied mother-in-law had knocked his lares and penates sky-high. After his solitary meal John sat at a front window.

He did not care to smoke. Outside the city roared to him to come join in its dance of folly and pleasure. The night was his. He might go forth unquestioned and thrum the strings of jollity as free as any gay bachelor there. He might carouse and wander and have his fling until dawn if he liked; and there would be no wrathful Katy waiting for him, bearing the chalice that held the dregs of his joy. He might

play pool at McCloskey's with his roistering friends
until Aurora dimmed the electric bulbs if he chose.
The hymeneal strings that had curbed him always
when the Frogmore flats had palled upon him were
loosened. Katy was gone.

John Perkins was not accustomed to analyzing his
emotions. But as he sat in his Katy-bereft 10x12
parlor he hit unerringly upon the keynote of his discomfort. He knew now that Katy was necessary to
his happiness. His feeling for her, lulled into uncon-
sciousness by the dull round of domesticity, had been
sharply stirred by the loss of her presence. Has it
not been dinned into us by proverb and sermon and
fable that we never prize the music till the sweet-
voiced bird has flown — or in other no less florid and
true utterances?

" I'm a double-dyed dub," mused John Perkins,
" the way I've been treating Katy. Off every night
playing pool and bumming with the boys instead of
staying home with her. The poor girl here all alone
with nothing to amuse her, and me acting that way!
John Perkins, you're the worst kind of a shine. I'm
going to make it up for the little girl. I'll take her
out and let her see some amusement. And I'll cut out
the McCloskey gang right from this minute."

Yes, there was the city roaring outside for John
Perkins to come dance in the train of Momus. And
at McCloskey's the boys were knocking the balls idly

[47]

into the pockets against the hour for the nightly game. But no primrose way nor clicking cue could woo the remorseful soul of Perkins the bereft. The thing that was his, lightly held and half scorned, had been taken away from him, and he wanted it. Backward to a certain man named Adam, whom the cherubim bounced from the orchard, could Perkins, the remorseful, trace his descent.

Near the right hand of John Perkins stood a chair. On the back of it stood Katy's blue shirtwaist. It still retained something of her contour. Midway of the sleeves were fine, individual wrinkles made by the movements of her arms in working for his comfort and pleasure. A delicate but impelling odor of bluebells came from it. John took it and looked long and soberly at the unresponsive grenadine. Katy had never been unresponsive. Tears:— yes, tears — came into John Perkins's eyes. When she came back things would be different. He would make up for all his neglect. What was life without her?

The door opened. Katy walked in carrying a little hand satchel. John stared at her stupidly.

" My! I'm glad to get back," said Katy. " Ma wasn't sick to amount to anything. Sam was at the depot, and said she just had a little spell, and got all right soon after they telegraphed. So I took the next train back. I'm just dying for a cup of coffee."

Nobody heard the click and the rattle of the cog-

wheels as the third-floor front of the Frogmore flats
buzzed its machinery back into the Order of Things.
A band slipped, a spring was touched, the gear was
adjusted and the wheels revolved in their old orbits.

John Perkins looked at the clock. It was 8.15.
He reached for his hat and walked to the door.

" Now, where are you going, I'd like to know, John
Perkins? " asked Katy, in a querulous tone.

" Thought I'd drop up to McCloskey's," said John,
" and play a game or two of pool with the fellows."

TWO THANKSGIVING DAY GENTLEMEN

THERE is one day that is ours. There is one day when all we Americans who are not self-made go back to the old home to eat saleratus biscuits and marvel how much nearer to the porch the old pump looks than it use to. Bless the day. President Roosevelt gives it to us. We hear some talk of the Puritans, but don't just remember who they were. Bet we can lick 'em, anyhow, if they try to land again. Plymouth Rocks? Well, that sounds more familiar. Lots of us have had to come down to hens since the Turkey Trust got its work in. Bet somebody in Washington is leaking out advance information to 'em about these Thanksgiving proclamations.

The big city east of the cranberry bogs has made Thanksgiving Day an institution. The last Thursday in November is the only day in the year on which it recognizes the part of America lying across the ferries. It is the one day that is purely American. Yes, a day of celebration, exclusively American.

And now for the story which is to prove to you that we have traditions on this side of the ocean that are becoming older at a much rapider rate than those

[50]

of England are — thanks to our git-up and enterprise.

Stuffy Pete took his seat on the third bench to the right as you enter Union Square from the east, at the walk opposite the fountain. Every Thanksgiving Day for nine years he had taken his seat there promptly at 1 o'clock. For every time he had done so things had happened to him — Charles Dickensy things that swelled his waistcoat above his heart, and equally on the other side.

But to-day Stuffy Pete's appearance at the annual trysting place seemed to have been rather the result of habit than of the yearly hunger which, as the philanthropists seem to think, afflicts the poor at such extended intervals.

Certainly Pete was not hungry. He had just come from a feast that had left him of his powers barely those of respiration and locomotion. His eyes were like two pale gooseberries firmly imbedded in a swollen and gravy-smeared mask of putty. His breath came in a short wheezes; a senatorial roll of adipose tissue denied a fashionable set to his upturned coat collar. Buttons that had been sewed upon his clothes by kind Salvation fingers a week before flew like popcorn, strewing the earth around him. Ragged he was, with a split shirt front open to the wishbone; but the November breeze, carrying fine snowflakes, brought him only a grateful coolness. For Stuffy Pete was

overcharged with the caloric produced by a super-
bountiful dinner, beginning with oysters and ending
with plum pudding, and including (it seemed to him)
all the roast turkey and baked potatoes and chicken
salad and squash pie and ice cream in the world.
Wherefore he sat, gorged, and gazed upon the world
with after-dinner contempt.

The meal had been an unexpected one. He was
passing a red brick mansion near the beginning of
Fifth avenue, in which lived two old ladies of ancient
family and a reverence for traditions. They even denied the existence of New York, and believed that
Thanksgiving Day was declared solely for Washington Square. One of their traditional habits was to
station a servant at the postern gate with orders to
admit the first hungry wayfarer that came along
after the hour of noon had struck, and banquet him to
a finish. Stuffy Pete happened to pass by on his way
to the park, and the seneschals gathered him in and
upheld the custom of the castle.

After Stuffy Pete had gazed straight before him
for ten minutes he was conscious of a desire for a
more varied field of vision. With a tremendous effort
he moved his head slowly to the left. And then his
eyes bulged out fearfully, and his breath ceased, and
the rought-shod ends of his short legs wriggled and
rustled on the gravel.

For the Old Gentleman was coming across Fourth avenue toward his bench.

Every Thanksgiving Day for nine years the Old Gentleman had come there and found Stuffy Pete on his bench. That was a thing that the Old Gentleman was trying to make a tradition of. Every Thanksgiving Day for nine years he had found Stuffy there, and had led him to a restaurant and watched him eat a big dinner. They do those things in England unconsciously. But this is a young country, and nine years is not so bad. The Old Gentleman was a staunch American patriot, and considered himself a pioneer in American tradition. In order to become picturesque we must keep on doing one thing for a long time without ever letting it get away from us. Something like collecting the weekly dimes in industrial insurance. Or cleaning the streets.

The Old Gentleman moved, straight and stately, toward the Institution that he was rearing. Truly, the annual feeding of Stuffy Pete was nothing national in its character, such as the Magna Charta or jam for breakfast was in England. But it was a step. It was almost feudal. It showed, at least, that a Custom was not impossible to New Y — ahem! — America.

The Old Gentleman was thin and tall and sixty. He was dressed all in black, and wore the old-fashioned kind of glasses that won't stay on your nose. His hair was whiter and thinner than it had been last year, and he seemed to make more use of his big, knobby cane with the crooked handle.

As his established benefactor came up Stuffy wheezed and shuddered like some woman's over-fat pug when a street dog bristles up at him. He would have flown, but all the skill of Santos-Dumont could not have separated him from his bench. Well had the myrmidons of the two old ladies done their work.

"Good morning," said the Old Gentleman. "I am glad to perceive that the vicissitudes of another year have spared you to move in health about the beautiful world. For that blessing alone this day of thanksgiving is well proclaimed to each of us. If you will come with me, my man, I will provide you with a dinner that should make your physical being accord with the mental."

That is what the Old Gentleman said every time. Every Thanksgiving Day for nine years. The words themselves almost formed an Institution. Nothing could be compared with them except the Declaration of Independence. Always before they had been music in Stuffy's ears. But now he looked up at the Old Gentleman's face with tearful agony in his own. The fine snow almost sizzled when it fell upon his perspiring brow. But the Old Gentleman shivered a little and turned his back to the wind.

Stuffy had always wondered why the Old Gentleman

spoke his speech rather sadly. He did not know that it was because he was wishing every time that he had a son to succeed him. A son who would come there after he was gone — a son who would stand proud and strong before some subsequent Stuffy, and say: "In memory of my father." Then it would be an Institution.

But the Old Gentleman had no relatives. He lived in rented rooms in one of the decayed old family brownstone mansions in one of the quiet streets east of the park. In the winter he raised fuschias in a little conservatory the size of a steamer trunk. In the spring he walked in the Easter parade. In the summer he lived at a farmhouse in the New Jersey hills, and sat in a wicker armchair, speaking of a butterfly, the ornithoptera amphrisius, that he hoped to find some day. In the autumn he fed Stuffy a dinner. These were the Old Gentleman's occupations.

Stuffy Pete looked up at him for a half minute, stewing and helpless in his own self-pity. The Old Gentleman's eyes were bright with the giving-pleasure. His face was getting more lined each year, but his little black necktie was in as jaunty a bow as ever, and his linen was beautiful and white, and his gray mustache was curled carefully at the ends. And then Stuffy made a noise that sounded like peas bubbling in a pot. Speech was intended; and as the Old Gentleman had heard the sounds nine times before, he rightly construed them into Stuffy's old formula of acceptance.

"Thankee, sir. I'll go with ye, and much obliged. I'm very hungry, sir."

The coma of repletion had not prevented from entering Stuffy's mind the conviction that he was the basis of an Institution. His Thanksgiving appetite was not his own; it belonged by all the sacred rights of established custom, if not by the actual Statute of Limitations, to this kind old gentleman who had preempted it. True, America is free; but in order to establish tradition some one must be a repetend — a repeating decimal. The heroes are not all heroes of steel and gold. See one here that wielded only weapons of iron, badly silvered, and tin.

The Old Gentleman led his annual protégé southward to the restaurant, and to the table where the feast had always occurred. They were recognized.

"Here comes de old guy," said a waiter, "dat blows dat same bum to a meal every Thanksgiving."

The Old Gentleman sat across the table glowing like a smoked pearl at his corner-stone of future ancient Tradition. The waiters heaped the table with holiday food — and Stuffy, with a sigh that was mistaken for hunger's expression, raised knife and fork and carved for himself a crown of imperishable bay.

No more valiant hero ever fought his way through the ranks of an enemy. Turkey, chops, soups, vegetables, pies, disappeared before him as fast as they could be served. Gorged nearly to the uttermost when he entered the restaurant, the smell of food had almost caused him to lose his honor as a gentleman, but he rallied like a true knight. He saw the look of beneficent happiness on the Old Gentleman's face — a happier look than even the fuschias and the ornithoptera amphrisius had ever brought to it — and he had not the heart to see it wane.

In an hour Stuffy leaned back with a battle won.

"Thankee kindly, sir," he puffed like a leaky steam pipe; "thankee kindly for a hearty meal."

Then he arose heavily with glazed eyes and started toward the kitchen. A waiter turned him about like a top, and pointed him toward the door. The Old Gentleman carefully counted out $1.30 in silver change, leaving three nickels for the waiter.

They parted as they did each year at the door, the Old Gentleman going south, Stuffy north.

Around the first corner Stuffy turned, and stood for one minute. Then he seemed to puff out his rags as an owl puffs out his feathers, and fell to the sidewalk like a sunstricken horse.

When the ambulance came the young surgeon and the driver cursed softly at his weight. There was no smell of whiskey to justify a transfer to the patrol wagon, so Stuffy and his two dinners went to the hospital. There they stretched him on a bed and began to test him for strange diseases, with the hope of getting a chance at some problem with the bare steel.

And lo! an hour later another ambulance brought the Old Gentleman. And they laid him on another bed and spoke of appendicitis, for he looked good for the bill.

But pretty soon one of the young doctors met one of the young nurses whose eyes he liked, and stopped to chat with her about the cases.

" That nice old gentleman over there, now," he said, " you wouldn't think that was a case of almost starvation. Proud old family, I guess. He told me he hadn't eaten a thing for three days."

THE ASSESSOR OF SUCCESS

HASTINGS BEAUCHAMP MORLEY sauntered across Union Square with a pitying look at the hundreds that lolled upon the park benches. They were a motley lot, he thought; the men with stolid, animal, unshaven faces; the women wriggling and self-conscious, twining and untwining their feet that hung four inches above the gravelled walks.

Were I Mr. Carnegie or Mr. Rockefeller I would put a few millions in my inside pocket and make an appointment with all the Park Commissioners (around the corner, if necessary), and arrange for benches in all the parks of the world low enough for women to sit upon, and rest their feet upon the ground. After that I might furnish libraries to towns that would pay, for 'em, or build sanitariums for crank professors, and call 'em colleges, if I wanted to.

Women's rights societies have been laboring for many years after equality with man. With what result? When they sit on a bench they must twist their ankles together and uncomfortably swing their highest French heels clear of earthly support. Begin at the bottom, ladies. Get your feet on the ground, and then rise to theories of mental equality.

Hastings Beauchamp Morley was carefully and neatly dressed. That was the result of an instinct due to his birth and breeding. It is denied us to look further into a man's bosom than the starch on his shirt front; so it is left to us only to recount his walks and conversation.

Morley had not a cent in his pockets; but he smiled pityingly at a hundred grimy, unfortunate ones who had no more, and who would have no more when the sun's first rays yellowed the tall paper-cutter building on the west side of the square. But Morley would have enough by then. Sundown had seen his pockets empty before; but sunrise had always seen them lined.

First he went to the house of a clergyman off Madison avenue and presented a forged letter of introduction that holily purported to issue from a pastorate in Indiana. This netted him $5 when backed up by a realistic romance of a delayed remittance.

On the sidewalk, twenty steps from the clergyman's door, a pale-faced, fat man huskily enveloped him with a raised, red fist and the voice of a bell buoy, demanding payment of an old score.

" Why, Bergman, man," sang Morley, dulcetly, " is this you? I was just on my way up to your place to settle up. That remittance from my aunt arrived only this morning. Wrong address was the trouble. Come up to the corner and I'll square up. Glad to see you. Saves me a walk."

Four drinks placated the emotional Bergman. There was an air about Morley when he was backed by money in hand that would have stayed off a call loan at Rothschilds'. When he was penniless his bluff was pitched half a tone lower, but few are competent to detect the difference in the notes.

"You gum to mine blace und bay me to-morrow, Mr. Morley," said Bergman. "Oxcuse me dat I dun you on der street. But I haf not seen you in dree mont'. Pros't!"

Morley walked away with a crooked smile on his pale, smooth face. The credulous, drink-softened German amused him. He would have to avoid Twenty-ninth street in the future. He had not been aware that Bergman ever went home by that route.

At the door of a darkened house two squares to the north Morley knocked with a peculiar sequence of raps. The door opened to the length of a six-inch chain, and the pompous, important black face of an African guardian imposed itself in the opening. Morley was admitted.

In a third-story room, in an atmosphere opaque with smoke, he hung for ten minutes above a roulette wheel. Then downstairs he crept, and was out-sped by the important negro, jingling in his pocket the 40 cents in silver that remained to him of his five-dollar capital. At the corner he lingered, undecided.

Across the street was a drug store well lighted,

sending forth gleams from the German silver and crystal of its soda fountain and glasses. Along came a youngster of five, headed for the dispensary, stepping high with the consequence of a big errand, possibly one to which his advancing age had earned him promotion. In his hand he clutched something tightly, publicly, proudly, conspicuously.

Morley stopped him with his winning smile and soft speech.

"Me?" said the youngster. "I'm doin' to the drug 'tore for mamma. She dave me a dollar to buy a bottle of med'cin."

"Now, now, now!" said Morley. "Such a big man you are to be doing errands for mamma. I must go along with my little man to see that the cars don't run over him. And on the way we'll have some chocolates. Or would he rather have lemon drops?"

Morley entered the drug store leading the child by the hand. He presented the prescription that had been wrapped around the money.

On his face was a smile, predatory, parental, politic, profound.

"Aqua pura, one pint," said he to the druggist. "Sodium chloride, ten grains. Fiat solution. And don't try to skin me, because I know all about the number of gallons of H_2O in the Croton reservoir, and I always use the other ingredient on my potatoes."

[62]

" Fifteen cents," said the druggist, with a wink, after he had compounded the order. " I see you understand pharmacy. A dollar is the regular price."

" To gulls," said Morley, smilingly.

He settled the wrapped bottle carefully in the child's arms and escorted him to the corner. In his own pocket he dropped the 85 cents accruing to him by virtue of his chemical knowledge.

" Look out for the cars, sonny," he said, cheerfully, to his small victim.

Two street cars suddenly swooped in opposite directions upon the youngster. Morley dashed between them and pinned the infantile messenger by the neck, holding him in safety. Then from the corner of his street he sent him on his way, swindled, happy, and sticky with vile, cheap candy from the Italian's fruit stand.

Morley went to a restaurant and ordered a sirloin and a pint of inexpensive Chateau Breuille. He laughed noiselessly, but so genuinely that the waiter ventured to premise that good news had come his way.

" Why, no," said Morley, who seldom held conversation with any one. " It is not that. It is something else that amuses me. Do you know what three divisions of people are easiest to over-reach in transactions of all kinds? "

" Sure," said the waiter, calculating the size of the tip promised by the careful knot of Morley's tie;

" there's the buyers from the dry goods stores in the South during August, and honeymooners from Staten Island, and " —

" Wrong! " said Morley, chuckling happily. " The answer is just — men, women and children. The world — well, say New York and as far as summer boarders can swim out from Long Island — is full of greenhorns. Two minutes longer on the broiler would have made this steak fit to be eaten by a gentleman, Francois."

" If yez t'inks it's on de bum," said the waiter, Oi'll " —

Morley lifted his hand in protest — slightly martyred protest.

" It will do," he said, magnanimously. " And now, green Chartreuse, frappe and a demi-tasse."

Morley went out leisurely and stood on a corner where two tradeful arteries of the city cross. With a solitary dime in his pocket, he stood on the curb watching with confident, cynical, smiling eyes the tides of people that flowed past him. Into that stream he must cast his net and draw fish for his further sustenance and need. Good Izaak Walton had not the half of his self reliance and bait-lore.

A joyful party of four — two women and two men — fell upon him with cries of delight. There was a dinner party on — where had he been for a fortnight past? — what luck to thus run upon him! They surrounded and engulfed him — he must join them — tra la la — and the rest.

One with a white hat plume curving to the shoulder touched his sleeve, and cast at the others a triumphant look that said: " See what I can do with him? " and added her queen's command to the invitations.

" I leave you to imagine," said Morley, pathetically, " how it desolates me to forego the pleasure. But my friend Carruthers, of the New York Yacht Club, is to pick me up here in his motor car at 8."

The white plume tossed, and the quartet danced like midges around an arc light down the frolicsome way.

Morley stood, turning over and over the dime in his pocket and laughing gleefully to himself.

" ' Front,' " he chanted under his breath; " ' front ' does it. It is trumps in the game. How they take it in! Men, women and children — forgeries, water-and-salt lies — how they all take it in! "

An old man with an ill-fitting suit, a straggling gray beard and a corpulent umbrella hopped from the conglomeration of cabs and street cars to the sidewalk at Morley's side.

" Stranger," said he, " excuse me for troubling you, but do you know anybody in this here town named Solomon Smothers? He's my son, and I've come down from Ellenville to visit him. Be darned if I know what I done with his street and number."

"I do not sir," said Morley, half closing his eyes to veil the joy in them. "You had better apply to the police."

"The police!" said the old man. "I ain't done nothin' to call in the police about. I just come down to see Ben. He lives in a five-story house, he writes me. If you know anybody by that name and could " —

"I told you I did not," said Morley, coldly. "I know no one by the name of Smithers, and I advise you to " —

"Smothers not Smithers," interrupted the old man hopefully. "A heavy-sot man, sandy complected, about twenty-nine, two front teeth out, about five foot " —

"Oh, 'Smothers!'" exclaimed Morley. "Sol Smothers? Why, he lives in the next house to me. I thought you said 'Smithers.'"

Morley looked at his watch. You must have a watch. You can do it for a dollar. Better go hungry than forego a gunmetal or the ninety-eight-cent one that the railroads — according to these watchmakers — are run by.

"The Bishop of Long Island," said Morley, "was to meet me here at 8 to dine with me at the Kingfishers' Club. But I can't leave the father of my friend Sol Smothers alone on the street. By St. Swithin, Mr. Smothers, we Wall street men have to work! Tired is no name for it! I was about to step across to the other corner and have a glass of ginger ale with a dash of sherry when you approached me. You must let me take you to Sol's house, Mr. Smothers. But before we take the car I hope you will join me in " —

An hour later Morley seated himself on the end of a quiet bench in Madison Square, with a twenty-five-cent cigar between his lips and $140 in deeply creased bills in his inside pocket. Content, light-hearted, ironical, keenly philosophic, he watched the moon drifting in and out amidst a maze of flying clouds. An old, ragged man with a low-bowed head sat at the other end of the bench.

Presently the old man stirred and looked at his bench companion. In Morley's appearance he seemed to recognize something superior to the usual nightly occupants of the benches.

" Kind sir," he whined, " if you could spare a dime or even a few pennies to one who " —

Morley cut short his stereotyped appeal by throwing him a dollar.

" God bless you! " said the old man. " I've been trying to find work for " —

" Work! " echoed Morley with his ringing laugh. " You are a fool, my friend. The world is a rock to you, no doubt; but you must be an Aaron and smite it with your rod. Then things better than water will gush out of it for you. That is what the world is for. It gives to me whatever I want from it."

"God has blessed you," said the old man. "It is only work that I have known. And now I can get no more."

"I must go home," said Morley, rising and buttoning his coat. "I stopped here only for a smoke. I hope you may find work."

"May your kindness be rewarded this night," said the old man.

"Oh," said Morley, "you have your wish already. I am satisfied. I think good luck follows me like a dog. I am for yonder bright hotel across the square for the night. And what a moon that is lighting up the city to-night. I think no one enjoys the moonlight and such little things as I do. Well, a good-night to you."

Morley walked to the corner where he would cross to his hotel. He blew slow streamers of smoke from his cigar heavenward. A policeman passing saluted to his benign nod. What a fine moon it was.

The clock struck nine as a girl just entering womanhood stopped on the corner waiting for the approaching car. She was hurrying as if homeward from employment or delay. Her eyes were clear and pure, she was dressed in simple white, she looked eagerly for the car and neither to the right nor the left.

Morley knew her. Eight years before he had sat

on the same bench with her at school. There had been no sentiment between them — nothing but the friendship of innocent days.

But he turned down the side street to a quiet spot and laid his suddenly burning face against the cool iron of a lamp-post, and said dully:

God! I wish I could die."

THE BUYER FROM CACTUS CITY

IT is well that hay fever and colds do not obtain in the healthful vicinity of Cactus City, Texas, for the dry goods emporium of Navarro & Platt, situated there, is not to be sneezed at.

Twenty thousand people in Cactus City scatter their silver coin with liberal hands for the things that their hearts desire. The bulk of this semiprecious metal goes to Navarro & Platt. Their huge brick building covers enough ground to graze a dozen head of sheep. You can buy of them a rattlesnake-skin necktie, an automobile or an eighty-five dollar, latest style, ladies' tan coat in twenty different shades. Navarro & Platt first introduced pennies west of the Colorado River. They had been ranchmen with business heads, who saw that the world did not necessarily have to cease its revolutions after free grass went out.

Every spring, Navarro, senior partner, fifty-five, half Spanish, cosmopolitan, able, polished, had " gone on " to New York to buy goods. This year he shied at taking up the long trail. He was undoubtedly growing older; and he looked at his watch several times a day before the hour came for his siesta.

[70]

" John," he said, to his junior partner, " you shall go on this year to buy the goods."

Platt looked tired.

" I'm told," said he, " that New York is a plumb dead town; but I'll go. I can take a whirl in San Antone for a few days on my way and have some fun."

Two weeks later a man in a Texas full dress suit — black frock coat, broad-brimmed soft white hat, and lay-down collar 3-4 inch high, with black, wrought iron necktie — entered the wholesale cloak and suit establishment of Zizzbaum & Son, on lower Broadway.

Old Zizzbaum had the eye of an osprey, the memory of an elephant and a mind that unfolded from him in three movements like the puzzle of the carpenter's rule. He rolled to the front like a brunette polar bear, and shook Platt's hand.

" And how is the good Mr. Navarro in Texas? " he said. " The trip was too long for him this year, so? We welcome Mr. Platt instead."

" A bull's eye," said Platt, " and I'd give forty acres of unirrigated Pecos County land to know how you did it."

" I knew," grinned Zizzbaum, " just as I know that the rainfall in El Paso for the year was 28.5 inches, or an increase of 15 inches, and that therefore Navarro & Platt will buy a $15,000 stock of suits this spring instead of $10,000, as in a dry year. But that will be to-morrow.   There is first a cigar in my private office that will remove from your mouth the taste of the ones you smuggle across the Rio Grande and like —because they are smuggled."

It was late in the afternoon and business for the day had ended, Zizzbaum left Platt with a half-smoked cigar, and came out of the private office to Son, who was arranging his diamond scarfpin before a mirror, ready to leave.

" Abey," he said, " you will have to take Mr. Platt around to-night and show him things.   They are customers for ten years.   Mr. Navarro and I we played chess every moment of spare time when he came. That is good, but Mr. Platt is a young man and this is his first visit to New York.   He should amuse easily."

" All right," said Abey, screwing the guard tightly on his pin.   " I'll take him on.   After he's seen the Flatiron and the head waiter at the Hotel Astor and heard the phonograph play ' Under the Old Apple Tree ' it'll be half past ten, and Mr. Texas will be ready to roll up in his blanket.   I've got a supper engagement at 11.30, but he'll be all to the Mrs. Winslow before then."

The next morning at 10 Platt walked into the store ready to do business.   He had a bunch of hyacinths pinned on his lapel.   Zizzbaum himself waited on him.

Navarro & Platt were good customers, and never failed to take their discount for cash.

" And what did you think of our little town? " asked Zizzbaum, with the fatuous smile of the Manhattanite.

" I shouldn't care to live in it," said the Texan. " Your son and I knocked around quite a little last night. You've got good water, but Cactus City is better lit up."

" We've got a few lights on Broadway, don't you think, Mr. Platt? "

" And a good many shadows," said Platt. " I think I like your horses best. I haven't seen a crowbait since I've been in town."

Zizzbaum led him upstairs to show the samples of suits.

" Ask Miss Asher to come," he said to a clerk.

Miss Asher came, and Platt, of Navarro & Platt, felt for the first time the wonderful bright light of romance and glory descend upon him. He stood still as a granite cliff above the cañon of the Colorado, with his wide-open eyes fixed upon her. She noticed his look and flushed a little, which was contrary to her custom.

Miss Asher was the crack model of Zizzbaum & Son. She was of the blond type known as " medium," and her measurements even went the required 38-25-42 standard a little better. She had been at Zizzbaum's two years, and knew her business. Her eye was bright, but cool; and had she chosen to match her gaze against the optic of the famed basilisk, that fabulous monster's gaze would have wavered and softened first. Incidentally, she knew buyers.

"Now, Mr. Platt," said Zizzbaum, "I want you to see these princess gowns in the light shades. They will be the thing in your climate. This first, if you please, Miss Asher."

Swiftly in and out of the dressing-room the prize model flew, each time wearing a new costume and looking more stunning with every change. She posed with absolute self-possession before the stricken buyer, who stood, tongue-tied and motionless, while Zizzbaum orated oilily of the styles. On the model's face was her faint, impersonal professional smile that seemed to cover something like weariness or contempt.

When the display was over Platt seemed to hesitate. Zizzbaum was a little anxious, thinking that his customer might be inclined to try elsewhere. But Platt was only looking over in his mind the best building sites in Cactus City, trying to select one on which to build a house for his wife-to-be — who was just then in the dressing-room taking off an evening gown of lavender and tulle.

"Take your time, Mr. Platt," said Zizzbaum. "Think it over to-night. You won't find anybody else meet our prices on goods like these. I'm afraid you're having a dull time in New York, Mr. Platt. A young man like you — of course, you miss the society of the ladies. Wouldn't you like a nice young lady to take out to dinner this evening? Miss Asher, now, is a very nice young lady; she will make it agreeable for you."

"Why, she doesn't know me," said Platt, wonderingly. "She doesn't know anything about me. Would she go? I'm not acquainted with her."

"Would she go?" repeated Zizzbaum, with uplifted eyebrows. "Sure, she would go. I will introduce you. Sure, she would go."

He called Miss Asher loudly.

She came, calm and slightly contemptuous, in her white shirt waist and plain black skirt.

"Mr. Platt would like the pleasure of your company to dinner this evening," said Zizzbaum, walking away.

"Sure," said Miss Asher, looking at the ceiling. "I'd be much pleased. Nine-eleven West Twentieth street. What time?"

"Say seven o'clock."

"All right, but please don't come ahead of time. I room with a school teacher, and she doesn't allow any gentlemen to call in the room. There isn't any parlor, so you'll have to wait in the hall. I'll be ready."

At half past seven Platt and Miss Asher sat at a table in a Broadway restaurant. She was dressed in a plain, filmy black. Platt didn't know that it was all a part of her day's work.

With the unobtrusive aid of a good waiter he managed to order a respectable dinner, minus the usual Broadway preliminaries.

Miss Asher flashed upon him a dazzling smile.

"Mayn't I have something to drink?" she asked.

"Why, certainly," said Platt. "Anything you want."

"A dry Martini," she said to the waiter.

When it was brought and set before her Platt reached over and took it away.

"What is this?" he asked.

"A cocktail, of course."

"I thought it was some kind of tea you ordered. This is liquor. You can't drink this. What is your first name?"

"To my intimate friends," said Miss Asher, freezingly, "it is 'Helen.'"

"Listen, Helen," said Platt, leaning over the table. "For many years every time the spring flowers blossomed out on the prairies I got to thinking of somebody that I'd never seen or heard of. I knew it was you the minute I saw you yesterday. I'm going back home to-morrow, and you're going with me. I know it, for I saw it in your eyes when you first looked at me. You needn't kick, for you've got to fall into line. Here's a little trick I picked out for you on my way over."

He flicked a two-carat diamond solitaire ring across the table. Miss Asher flipped it back to him with her fork.

" Don't get fresh," she said, severely.

" I'm worth a hundred thousand dollars," said Platt. " I'll build you the finest house in West Texas."

" You can't buy me, Mr. Buyer," said Miss Asher, " if you had a hundred million. I didn't think I'd have to call you down. You didn't look like the others to me at first, but I see you're all alike."

" All who? " asked Platt.

" All you buyers. You think because we girls have to go out to dinner with you or lose our jobs that you're privileged to say what you please. Well, forget it. I thought you were different from the others, but I see I was mistaken."

Platt struck his fingers on the table with a gesture of sudden, illuminating satisfaction.

" I've got it! " he exclaimed, almost hilariously — " the Nicholson place, over on the north side. There's a big grove of live oaks and a natural lake. The old house can be pulled down and the new one set further back."

" Put out your pipe," said Miss Asher. " I'm sorry to wake you up, but you fellows might as well get wise, once for all, to where you stand. I'm supposed to go to dinner with you and help jolly you along so you'll trade with old Zizzy, but don't expect to find me in any of the suits you buy."

"Do you mean to tell me," said Platt, "that you go out this way with customers, and they all — they all talk to you like I have?"

"They all make plays," said Miss Asher. "But I must say that you've got 'em beat in one respect. They generally talk diamonds, while you've actually dug one up."

"How long have you been working, Helen?"

"Got my name pat, haven't you? I've been supporting myself for eight years. I was a cash girl and a wrapper and then a shop girl until I was grown, and then I got to be a suit model. Mr. Texas Man, don't you think a little wine would make this dinner a little less dry?"

"You're not going to drink wine any more, dear. It's awful to think how —— I'll come to the store to-morrow and get you. I want you to pick out an automobile before we leave. That's all we need to buy here."

"Oh, cut that out. If you knew how sick I am of hearing such talk."

After the dinner they walked down Broadway and came upon Diana's little wooded park. The trees caught Platt's eye at once, and he must turn along under the winding walk beneath them. The lights shone upon two bright tears in the model's eyes.

"I don't like that," said Platt. "What's the matter?"

"Don't you mind," said Miss Asher. "Well, it's because — well, I didn't think you were that kind when I first saw you. But you are all alike. And now will you take me home, or will I have to call a cop?"

Platt took her to the door of her boarding-house. They stood for a minute in the vestibule. She looked at him with such scorn in her eyes that even his heart of oak began to waver. His arm was half way around her waist, when she struck him a stinging blow on the face with her open hand.

As he stepped back a ring fell from somewhere and bounded on the tiled floor. Platt groped for it and found it.

"Now, take your useless diamond and go, Mr. Buyer," she said.

"This was the other one — the wedding ring," said the Texan, holding the smooth gold band on the palm of his hand.

Miss Asher's eyes blazed upon him in the half darkness.

"Was that what you meant?— did you "—

Somebody opened the door from inside the house.

"Good-night," said Platt. "I'll see you at the store to-morrow."

Miss Asher ran up to her room and shook the school teacher until she sat up in bed ready to scream " Fire ! "

" Where is it ? " she cried.

" That's what I want to know," said the model. " You've studied geography, Emma, and you ought to know. Where is a town called Cac — Cac — Carac — Caracas City, I think they called it ? "

" How dare you wake me up for that ? " said the school teacher. " Caracas is in Venezuela, of course."

" What's it like ? "

" Why, it's principally earthquakes and negroes and monkeys and malarial fever and volcanoes."

" I don't care," said Miss Asher, blithely; " I'm going there to-morrow."

THE BADGE OF POLICEMAN O'ROON

IT cannot be denied that men and women have looked
upon one another for the first time and become instantly enamored. It is a risky process, this love at
first sight, before she has seen him in Bradstreet or he
has seen her in curl papers. But these things do happen; and one instance must form a theme for this
story — though not, thank Heaven, to the overshad-
owing of more vital and important subjects, such as
drink, policemen, horses and earldoms.

During a certain war a troop calling itself the Gentle Riders rode into history and one or two ambuscades.
The Gentle Riders were recruited from the aristocracy of the wild men of the West and the wild men
of the aristocracy of the East. In khaki there is little
telling them one from another, so they became good
friends and comrades all around.

Ellsworth Remsen, whose old Knickerbocker descent
atoned for his modest rating at only ten millions, ate
his canned beef gayly by the campfires of the Gentle
Riders. The war was a great lark to him, so that he
scarcely regretted polo and planked shad.

One of the troopers was a well set up, affable, cool
young man, who called himself O'Roon. To this

[81]

young man Remsen took an especial liking. The two rode side by side during the famous mooted up-hill charge that was disputed so hotly at the time by the Spaniards and afterward by the Democrats.

After the war Remsen came back to his polo and shad. One day a well set up, affable, cool young man disturbed him at his club, and he and O'Roon were soon pounding each other and exchanging opprobious epithets after the manner of long-lost friends. O'Roon looked seedy and out of luck and perfectly contented. But it seemed that his content was only apparent.

"Get me a job, Remsen," he said. "I've just handed a barber my last shilling."

"No trouble at all," said Remsen. "I know a lot of men who have banks and stores and things downtown. Any particular line you fancy?"

"Yes," said O'Roon, with a look of interest. "I took a walk in your Central Park this morning. I'd like to be one of those bobbies on horseback. That would be about the ticket. Besides, it's the only thing I could do. I can ride a little and the fresh air suits me. Think you could land that for me?"

Remsen was sure that he could. And in a very short time he did. And they who were not above looking at mounted policemen might have seen a well set up, affable, cool young man on a prancing chestnut

[82]

steed attending to his duties along the driveways of
the park.

And now at the extreme risk of wearying old gentlemen who carry leather fob chains, and elderly ladies
who — but no! grandmother herself yet thrills at
foolish, immortal Romeo — there must be a hint of
love at first sight.

It came just as Remsen was strolling into Fifth
avenue from his club a few doors away.

A motor car was creeping along foot by foot, im-
peded by a freshet of vehicles that filled the street.
In the car was a chauffeur and an old gentleman with
snowy side whiskers and a Scotch plaid cap which
could not be worn while automobiling except by a personage. Not even a wine agent would dare to do it.
But these two were of no consequence — except, perhaps, for the guiding of the machine and the paying
for it. At the old gentleman's side sat a young lady
more beautiful than pomegranate blossoms, more ex-
quisite than the first quarter moon viewed at twilight
through the tops of oleanders. Remsen saw her and
knew his fate. He could have flung himself under
the very wheels that conveyed her, but he knew that
would be the last means of attracting the attention
of those who ride in motor cars. Slowly the auto
passed, and, if we place the poets above the autoists,
carried the heart of Remsen with it. Here was a
large city of millions, and many women who at a

certain distance appear to resemble pomegranate blossoms Yet he hoped to see her again; for each one fancies that his romance has its own tutelary guardian and divinity.

Luckily for Remsen's peace of mind there came a diversion in the guise of a reunion of the Gentle Riders of the city. There were not many of them — perhaps a score — and there was wassail, and things to eat, and speeches and the Spaniard was bearded again in recapitulation. And when daylight threatened them the survivors prepared to depart. But some remained upon the battlefield. One of these was Trooper O'Roon, who was not seasoned to potent liquids. His legs declined to fulfil the obligations they had sworn to the police department.

" I'm stewed, Remsen," said O'Roon to his friend. " Why do they built hotels that go round and round like catherine wheels? They'll take away my shield and break me. I can think and talk con-con-consec-sec-secutively, but I s-s-stammer with my feet. I've got to go on duty in three hours. The jig is up, Remsen. The jig is up, I tell you."

" Look at me," said Remsen, who was his smiling self, pointing to his own face; " whom do you see here? "

" Goo' fellow," said O'Roon, dizzily, " Goo' old Remsen."

" Not so,' said Remsen. " You see Mounted Po-

liceman O'Roon. Look at your face — no; you can't
do that without a glass — but look at mine, and think
of yours. How much alike are we? As two French
table d'hote dinners. With your badge, on your
horse, in your uniform, will I charm nurse-maids and
prevent the grass from growing under people's feet
in the Park this day. I will save your badge and
your honor, besides having the jolliest lark I've been
blessed with since we licked Spain.

Promptly on time the counterfeit presentment of
Mounted Policeman O'Roon single-footed into the
Park on his chestnut steed. In a uniform two men
who are unlike will look alike; two who somewhat resemble each other in feature and figure will appear as
twin brothers. So Remsen trotted down the bridle
paths, enjoying himself hugely, so few real pleasures
do ten-millionaires have.

Along the driveway in the early morning spun a
victoria drawn by a pair of fiery bays. There was
something foreign about the affair, for the Park is
rarely used in the morning except by unimportant
people who love to be healthy, poor and wise. In the
vehicle sat an old gentleman with snowy side-whiskers
and a Scotch plaid cap which could not be worn while
driving except by a personage. At his side sat the
lady of Remsen's heart — the lady who looked like
pomegranate blossoms and the gibbous moon.

Remsen met them coming. At the instant of their

[85]

passing her eyes looked into his, and but for the ever coward heart of a true lover he could have sworn that she flushed a faint pink. He trotted on for twenty yards, and then wheeled his horse at the sound of runaway hoofs. The bays had bolted.

Remsen sent his chestnut after the victoria like a shot. There was work cut out for the impersonator of Policeman O'Roon. The chestnut ranged alongside the off bay thirty seconds after the chase began, rolled his eye back at Remsen, and said in the only manner open to policemen's horses:

" Well, you duffer, are you going to do your share? You're not O'Roon, but it seems to me if you'd lean to the right you could reach the reins of that foolish, slow-running bay — ah! you're all right; O'Roon couldn't have done it more neatly!"

The runaway team was tugged to an inglorious halt by Remsen's tough muscles. The driver released his hands from the wrapped reins, jumped from his seat and stood at the heads of the team. The chestnut, approving his new rider, danced and pranced, reviling equinely the subdued bays. Remsen, lingering, was dimly conscious of a vague, impossible, unnecessary old gentleman in a Scotch cap who talked incessantly about something. And he was acutely conscious of a pair of violet eyes that would have drawn Saint Pyrites from his iron pillar — or whatever the allusion is — and of the lady's smile and look — a little frightened, but a look that, with the ever coward heart of a true lover, he could not yet construe. They were asking his name and bestowing upon him well-bred thanks for his heroic deed, and the Scotch cap was especially babbling and insistent. But the eloquent appeal was in the eyes of the lady.

A little thrill of satisfaction ran through Remsen, because he had a name to give which, without undue pride, was worthy of being spoken in high places, and a small fortune which, with due pride, he could leave at his end without disgrace.

He opened his lips to speak, and closed them again.

Who was he? Mounted Policeman O'Roon. The badge and the honor of his comrade were in his hands. If Ellsworth Remsen, ten-millionaire and Knickerbocker, had just rescued pomegranate blossoms and Scotch cap from possible death, where was Policeman O'Roon? Off his beat, exposed, disgraced, discharged. Love had come, but before that there had been something that demanded precedence — the fellowship of men on battlefields fighting an alien foe.

Remsen touched his cap, looked between the chestnut's ears, and took refuge in vernacularity.

" Don't mention it," he said stolidly. " We policemen are paid to do these things. It's our duty."

And he rode away — rode away cursing *noblesse oblige*, but knowing he could never have done anything else.

At the end of the day Remsen sent the chestnut to his stable and went to O'Roon's room. The policeman was again a well set up, affable, cool young man who sat by the window smoking cigars.

" I wish you and the rest of the police force and all badges, horses, brass buttons and men who can't drink two glasses of *brut* without getting upset were at the devil," said Remsen feelingly.

O'Roon smiled with evident satisfaction.

" Good old Remsen," he said, affably, " I know all about it. They trailed me down and cornered me here two hours ago. There was a little row at home, you know, and I cut sticks just to show them. I don't believe I told you that my Governor was the Earl of Ardsley. Funny you should bob against them in the Park. If you damaged that horse of mine I'll never forgive you. I'm going to buy him and take him back with me. Oh, yes, and I think my sister — Lady Angela, you know — wants particularly for you to come up to the hotel with me this evening. Didn't lose my badge, did you, Remsen? I've got to turn that in at Headquarters when I resign."

BRICKDUST ROW

BLINKER was displeased. A man of less culture and poise and wealth would have sworn. But Blinker always remembered that he was a gentleman — a thing that no gentleman should do. So he merely looked bored and sardonic while he rode in a hansom to the center of disturbance, which was the Broadway office of Lawyer Oldport, who was agent for the Blinker estate.

"I don't see," said Blinker, "why I should be always signing confounded papers. I am packed, and was to have left for the North Woods this morning. Now I must wait until to-morrow morning. I hate night trains. My best razors are, of course, at the bottom of some unidentifiable trunk. It is a plot to drive me to bay rum and a monologueing, thumb-handed barber. Give me a pen that doesn't scratch. I hate pens that scratch."

"Sit down," said double-chinned, gray Lawyer Oldport. "The worst has not been told you. Oh, the hardships of the rich! The papers are not yet ready to sign. They will be laid before you to-morrow at eleven. You will miss another day. Twice shall the barber tweak the helpless nose of a Blinker. Be thankful that your sorrows do not embrace a hair-cut."

"If," said Blinker, rising, "the act did not involve more signing of papers I would take my business out of your hands at once. Give me a cigar, please."

"If," said Lawyer Oldport, "I had cared to see an old friend's son gulped down at one mouthful by sharks I would have ordered you to take it away long ago. Now, let's quit fooling, Alexander. Besides the grinding task of signing your name some thirty times to-morrow, I must impose upon you the consideration of a matter of business — of business, and I may say humanity or right. I spoke to you about this five years ago, but you would not listen — you were in a hurry for a coaching trip, I think. The subject has come up again. The property —"

"Oh, property!" interrupted Blinker. "Dear Mr. Oldport, I think you mentioned to-morrow. Let's have it all at one dose to-morrow — signatures and property and snappy rubber bands and that smelly sealing-wax and all. Have luncheon with me? Well, I'll try to remember to drop in at eleven to-morrow. Morning."

The Blinker wealth was in lands, tenements and hereditaments, as the legal phrase goes. Lawyer Oldport had once taken Alexander in his little pulmonary gasoline runabout to see the many buildings and rows of buildings that he owned in the city. For Alexander was sole heir. They had amused Blinker very

[90]

much. The houses looked so incapable of producing the big sums of money that Lawyer Oldport kept piling up in banks for him to spend.

In the evening Blinker went to one of his clubs, intending to dine. Nobody was there except some old fogies playing whist who spoke to him with grave politeness and glared at him with savage contempt. Everybody was out of town. But here he was kept in like a schoolboy to write his name over and over on pieces of paper. His wounds were deep.

Blinker turned his back on the fogies, and said to the club steward who had come forward with some nonsense about cold fresh salmon roe:

"Symons, I'm going to Coney Island." He said it as one might say: "All's off; I'm going to jump into the river."

The joke pleased Symons. He laughed within a sixteenth of a note of the audibility permitted by the laws governing employees.

"Certainly, sir," he tittered. "Of course, sir, I think I can see you at Coney, Mr. Blinker."

Blinker got a paper and looked up the movements of Sunday steamboats. Then he found a cab at the first corner and drove to a North River pier. He stood in line, as democratic as you or I, and bought a ticket, and was trampled upon and shoved forward until, at last, he found himself on the upper deck of the boat staring brazenly at a girl who sat alone upon a camp stool. But Blinker did not intend to be brazen; the girl was so wonderfully good looking that he forgot for one minute that he was the prince incog, and behaved just as he did in society.

She was looking at him, too, and not severely. A puff of wind threatened Blinker's straw hat. He caught it warily and settled it again. The movement gave the effect of a bow. The girl nodded and smiled, and in another instant he was seated at her side. She was dressed all in white, she was paler than Blinker imagined milkmaids and girls of humble stations to be, but she was as tidy as a cherry blossom, and her steady, supremely frank gray eyes looked out from the intrepid depths of an unshadowed and untroubled soul.

" How dare you raise your hat to me? " she asked, with a smile-redeemed severity.

" I didn't," Blinker said, but he quickly covered the mistake by extending it to " I didn't know how to keep from it after I saw you."

" I do not allow gentlemen to sit by me to whom I have not been introduced," she said, with a sudden haughtiness that deceived him. He rose reluctantly, but her clear, teasing laugh brought him down to his chair again.

" I guess you weren't going far," she declared, with beauty's magnificent self-confidence.

" Are you going to Coney Island? " asked Blinker.

" Me? " She turned upon him wide-open eyes full of bantering surprise. " Why, what a question! Can't you see that I'm riding a bicycle in the park? " Her drollery took the form of impertinence.

" And I am laying brick on a tall factory chimney," said Blinker. " Mayn't we see Coney together? I'm all alone and I've never been there before."

" It depends," said the girl, " on how nicely you behave. " I'll consider your application until we get there."

Blinker took pains to provide against the rejection of his application. He strove to please. To adopt the metaphor of his nonsensical phrase, he laid brick upon brick on the tall chimney of his devoirs until, at length, the structure was stable and complete. The manners of the best society come around finally to simplicity; and as the girl's way was that naturally, they were on a mutual plane of communication from the beginning.

He learned that she was twenty, and her name was Florence; that she trimmed hats in a millinery shop; that she lived in a furnished room with her best chum Ella, who was cashier in a shoe store; and that a glass of milk from the bottle on the window-sill and an egg that boils itself while you twist up your hair makes a breakfast good enough for any one. Florence laughed when she heard " Blinker."

" Well," she said. " It certainly shows that you

have imagination. It gives the ' Smiths ' a chance for a little rest, anyhow."

They landed at Coney, and were dashed on the crest of a great human wave of mad pleasure-seekers into the walks and avenues of Fairyland gone into vaudeville.

With a curious eye, a critical mind and a fairly withheld judgment Blinker considered the temples, pagodas and kiosks of popularized delights. Hoi polloi trampled, hustled and crowded him. Basket parties bumped him; sticky children tumbled, howling, under his feet, candying his clothes. Insolent youths strolling among the booths with hard-won canes under one arm and easily won girls on the other, blew defiant smoke from cheap cigars into his face. The publicity gentlemen with megaphones, each before his own stupendous attraction, roared like Niagara in his ears. Music of all kinds that could be tortured from brass, reed, hide or string, fought in the air to gain space for its vibrations against its competitors. But what held Blinker in awful fascination was the mob, the multitude, the proletariat shrieking, struggling, hurrying, panting, hurling itself in incontinent frenzy, with unabashed abandon, into the ridiculous sham palaces of trumpery and tinsel pleasures. The vulgarity of it, its brutal overriding of all the tenets of repression and taste that were held by his caste, repelled him strongly.

In the midst of his disgust he turned and looked down at Florence by his side. She was ready with her quick smile and upturned, happy eyes, as bright and clear as the water in trout pools. The eyes were saying that they had the right to be shining and happy, for was their owner not with her (for the present) Man, her Gentleman Friend and holder of the keys to the enchanted city of fun?

Blinker did not read her look accurately, but by some miracle he suddenly saw Coney aright.

He no longer saw a mass of vulgarians seeking gross joys. He now looked clearly upon a hundred thousand true idealists. Their offenses were wiped out. Counterfeit and false though the garish joys of these spangled temples were, he perceived that deep under the gilt surface they offered saving and apposite balm and satisfaction to the restless human heart. Here, at least, was the husk of Romance, the empty but shining casque of Chivalry, the breath-catching though safe-guarded dip and flight of Adventure, the magic carpet that transports you to the realms of fairyland, though its journey be through but a few poor yards of space. He no longer saw a rabble, but his brothers seeking the ideal. There was no magic of poesy here or of art; but the glamour of their imagination turned yellow calico into cloth of gold and the megaphones into the silver trumpets of joy's heralds.

Almost humbled, Blinker rolled up the shirt sleeves of his mind and joined the idealists.

"You are the lady doctor," he said to Florence. "How shall we go about doing this jolly conglomeration of fairy tales, incorporated?"

"We will begin there," said the Princess, pointing to a fun pagoda on the edge of the sea, "and we will take them all in, one by one."

They caught the eight o'clock returning boat and sat, filled with pleasant fatigue against the rail in the bow, listening to the Italians' fiddle and harp. Blinker had thrown off all care. The North Woods seemed to him an uninhabitable wilderness. What a fuss he had made over signing his name — pooh! he could sign it a hundred times. And her name was as pretty as she was — "Florence," he said it to himself a great many times.

As the boat was nearing its pier in the North River a two-funnelled, drab, foreign-looking sea-going steamer was dropping down toward the bay. The boat turned its nose in toward its slip. The steamer veered as if to seek midstream, and then yawed, seemed to increase its speed and struck the Coney boat on the side near the stern, cutting into it with a terrifying shock and crash.

While the six hundred passengers on the boat were mostly tumbling about the decks in a shrieking panic the captain was shouting at the steamer that it should

not back off and leave the rent exposed for the water
to enter. But the steamer tore its way out like a
savage sawfish and cleaved its heartless way, full speed
ahead.

The boat began to sink at its stern, but moved
slowly toward the slip. The passengers were a fran-
tic mob, unpleasant to behold.

Blinker held Forence tightly until the boat had
righted itself. She made no sound or sign of fear.
He stood on a camp stool, ripped off the slats above
his head and pulled down a number of the life pre-
servers. He began to buckle one around Florence.
The rotten canvas split and the fraudulent granu-
lated cork came pouring out in a stream. Florence
caught a handful of it and laughed gleefully.

"It looks like breakfast food," she said. "Take it
off. They're no good."

She unbuckled it and threw it on the deck. She
made Blinker sit down, and sat by his side and put
her hand in his. "What'll you bet we don't reach the
pier all right?" she said, and began to hum a song.

And now the captain moved among the passengers
and compelled order. The boat would undoubtedly
make her slip, he said, and ordered the women and
children to the bow, where they could land first. The
boat, very low in the water at the stern, tried gallantly
to make his promise good.

" Florence," said Blinker, as she held him close by, an arm and hand, " I love you."

" That's what they all say," she replied, lightly.

" I am not one of ' they all,' " he persisted. " I never knew any one I could love before. I could pass my life with you and be happy every day. I am rich. I can make things all right for you."

" That's what they all say," said the girl again, weaving the words into her little, reckless song.

" Don't say that again," said Blinker in a tone that made her look at him in frank surprise.

" Why shouldn't I say it? " she asked calmly. " They all do."

" Who are ' they? ' " he asked, jealous for the first time in his existence.

" Why, the fellows I know."

" Do you know so many? "

" Oh, well, I'm not a wall flower," she answered with modest complacency.

" Where do you see these — these men? At your home? "

" Of course not. I meet them just as I did you. Sometimes on the boat, sometimes in the park, sometimes on the street. I'm a pretty good judge of a man. I can tell in a minute if a fellow is one who is likely to get fresh."

" What do you mean by ' fresh? ' "

" Why, try to kiss you — me, I mean."

[98]

" Do any of them try that? " asked Blinker, clench-
ing his teeth.

" Sure.   All men do.   You know that."

" Do you allow them? "

" Some.   Not many.   They won't take you out
anywhere unless you do."

She turned her head and looked searchingly at
Blinker.   Her eyes were as innocent as a child's.
There was a puzzled look in them, as though she did
not understand him.

" What's wrong about my meeting fellows? " she
asked, wonderingly.

" Everything," he answered, almost savagely.
" Why don't you entertain your company in the house
where you live?   Is it necessary to pick up Tom, Dick
and Harry on the streets? "

She kept her absolutely ingenuous eyes upon his.

" If you could see the place where I live you
wouldn't ask that.   I live in Brickdust Row.   They
call it that because there's red dust from the bricks
crumbling over everything.   I've lived there for more
than four years.   There's no place to receive company.   You can't have anybody come to your room.
What else is there to do?   A girl has got to meet the
men, hasn't she? "

" Yes," he said, hoarsely.   " A girl has got to meet
a — has got to meet the men."

" The first time one spoke to me on the street," she

continued, " I ran home and cried all night. But you get used to it. I meet a good many nice fellows at church. I go on rainy days and stand in the vestibule until one comes up with an umbrella. I wish there was a parlor, so I could ask you to call, Mr. Blinker — are you really sure it isn't ' Smith,' now? "

The boat landed safely. Blinker had a confused impression of walking with the girl through quiet crosstown streets until she stopped at a corner and held out her hand.

" I live just one more block over," she said. " Thank you for a very pleasant afternoon."

Blinker muttered something and plunged north-ward till he found a cab. A big, gray church loomed slowly at his right. Blinker shook his fist at it through the window.

" I gave you a thousand dollars last week," he cried under his breath, " and she meets them in your very doors. There is something wrong; there is something wrong."

At eleven the next day Blinker signed his name thirty times with a new pen provided by Lawyer Old-port.

" Now let me go to the woods," he said surlily.

" You are not looking well," said Lawyer Oldport. " The trip will do you good. But listen, if you will, to that little matter of business of which I spoke to you yesterday, and also five years ago. There are some buildings, fifteen in number, of which there are new five-year leases to be signed. Your father contemplated a change in the lease provisions, but never made it. He intended that the parlors of these houses should not be sub-let, but that the tenants should be allowed to use them for reception rooms. These houses are in the shopping district, and are mainly tenanted by young working girls. As it is they are forced to seek companionship outside. This row of red brick —"

Blinker interrupted him with a loud, discordant laugh.

" Brickdust Row for an even hundred," he cried. " And I own it. Have I guessed right? "

" The tenants have some such name for it,'" said Lawyer Oldport.

Blinker arose and jammed his hat down to his eyes.

" Do what you please with it," he said harshly. " Remodel it, burn it, raze it to the ground. But, man, it's too late I tell you. It's too late. It's too late. It's too late."

THE MAKING OF A NEW YORKER

BESIDES many other things, Raggles was a poet.
He was called a tramp; but that was only an elliptical
way of saying that he was a philosopher, an artist, a
traveller, a naturalist and a discoverer. But most
of all he was a poet. In all his life he never wrote a
line of verse; he lived his poetry. His Odyssey
would have been a Limerick, had it been written.
But, to linger with the primary proposition, Raggles
was a poet.

Raggles's specialty, had he been driven to ink and
paper, would have been sonnets to the cities. He
studied cities as women study their reflections in mir-
rors; as children study the glue and sawdust of a
dislocated doll; as the men who write about wild animals study the cages in the zoo. A city to Raggles
was not merely a pile of bricks and mortar, peopled
by a certain number of inhabitants; it was a thing
with a soul characteristic and distinct; an individual
conglomeration of life, with its own peculiar essence,
flavor and feeling. Two thousand miles to the north
and south, east and west, Raggles wandered in poetic
fervor, taking the cities to his breast. He footed it
on dusty roads, or sped magnificently in freight cars,

counting time as of no account. And when he had found the heart of a city and listened to its secret confession, he strayed on, restless, to another. Fickle Raggles! — but perhaps he had not met the civic corporation that could engage and hold his critical fancy.

Through the ancient poets we have learned that the cities are feminine. So they were to poet Raggles; and his mind carried a concrete and clear conception of the figure that symbolized and typified each one that he had wooed.

Chicago seemed to swoop down upon him with a breezy suggestion of Mrs. Partington, plumes and patchouli, and to disturb his rest with a soaring and beautiful song of future promise. But Raggles would awake to a sense of shivering cold and a haunting impression of ideals lost in a depressing aura of potato salad and fish.

Thus Chicago affected him. Perhaps there is a vagueness and inaccuracy in the description; but that is Raggles's fault. He should have recorded his sensations in magazine poems.

Pittsburg impressed him as the play of " Othello " performed in the Russian language in a railroad station by Dockstader's minstrels. A royal and generous lady this Pittsburg, though — homely, hearty, with flushed face, washing the dishes in a silk dress and white kid slippers, and bidding Raggles sit be-

[103]

fore the roaring fireplace and drink champagne with his pigs' feet and fried potatoes.

New Orleans had simply gazed down upon him from a balcony. He could see her pensive, starry eyes and catch the flutter of her fan, and that was all. Only once he came face to face with her. It was at dawn, when she was flushing the red bricks of the banquette with a pail of water. She laughed and hummed a chansonette and filled Raggles's shoes with ice-cold water. Allons!

Boston construed herself to the poetic Raggles in an erratic and singular way. It seemed to him that he had drunk cold tea and that the city was a white, cold cloth that had been bound tightly around his brow to spur him to some unknown but tremendous mental effort. And, after all, he came to shovel snow for a livelihood; and the cloth, becoming wet, tightened its knots and could not be removed.

Indefinite and unintelligible ideas, you will say; but your disapprobation should be tempered with gratitude, for these are poets' fancies — and suppose you had come upon them in verse!

One day Raggles came and laid siege to the heart of the great city of Manhattan. She was the greatest of all; and he wanted to learn her note in the scale; to taste and appraise and classify and solve and label her and arrange her with the other cities that had given him up the secret of their individuality. And here we cease to be Raggles's translator and become his chronicler.

Raggles landed from a ferry-boat one morning and walked into the core of the town with the blasé air of a cosmopolite. He was dressed with care to play the role of an "unidentified man." No country, race, class, clique, union, party, clan or bowling association could have claimed him. His clothing, which had been donated to him piece-meal by citizens of different height, but same number of inches around the heart, was not yet as uncomfortable to his figure as those specimens of raiment, self-measured, that are railroaded to you by transcontinental tailors with a suit case, suspenders, silk handkerchief and pearl studs as a bonus. Without money — as a poet should be — but with the ardor of an astronomer discovering a new star in the chorus of the milky way, or a man who has seen ink suddenly flow from his fountain pen, Raggles wandered into the great city.

Late in the afternoon he drew out of the roar and commotion with a look of dumb terror on his countenance. He was defeated, puzzled, discomfited, frightened. Other cities had been to him as long primer to read; as country maidens quickly to fathom; as send-price-of-subscription-with-answer rebuses to solve; as oyster cocktails to swallow; but here was one as cold, glittering, serene, impossible as a four-carat diamond in a window to a lover outside fingering damply in his pocket his ribbon-counter salary.

The greetings of the other cities he had known — their homespun kindliness, their human gamut of rough charity, friendly curses, garrulous curiosity and easily estimated credulity or indifference. This city of Manhattan gave him no clue; it was walled against him. Like a river of adamant it flowed past him in the streets. Never an eye was turned upon him; no voice spoke to him. His heart yearned for the clap of Pittsburg's sooty hand on his shoulder; for Chicago's menacing but social yawp in his ear; for the pale and eleemosynary stare through the Bostonian eyeglass — even for the precipitate but unmalicious boot-toe of Louisville or St. Louis.

On Broadway Raggles, successful suitor of many cities, stood, bashful, like any country swain. For the first time he experienced the poignant humiliation of being ignored. And when he tried to reduce this brilliant, swiftly changing, ice-cold city to a formula he failed utterly. Poet though he was, it offered him no color, no similes, no points of comparison, no flaw in its polished facets, no handle by which he could hold it up and view its shape and structure, as he familiarly and often contemptuously had done with other towns. The houses were interminable ramparts loopholed for defense; the people were bright but bloodless spectres passing in sinister and selfish array.

THE MAKING OF A NEW YORKER

The thing that weighed heaviest on Raggles's soul and clogged his poet's fancy was the spirit of absolute egotism that seemed to saturate the people as toys are saturated with paint. Each one that he considered appeared a monster of abominable and insolent conceit. Humanity was gone from them; they were toddling idols of stone and varnish, worshipping themselves and greedy for though oblivious of worship from their fellow graven images. Frozen, cruel, implacable, impervious, cut to an identical pattern, they hurried on their ways like statues brought by some miracles to motion, while soul and feeling lay unaroused in the reluctant marble.

Gradually Raggles became conscious of certain types. One was an elderly gentleman with a snow-white, short beard, pink, unwrinkled face and stony, sharp blue eyes, attired in the fashion of a gilded youth, who seemed to personify the city's wealth, ripeness and frigid unconcern. Another type was a woman, tall, beautiful, clear as a steel engraving, goddess-like, calm, clothed like the princesses of old, with eyes as coldly blue as the reflection of sunlight on a glacier. And another was a by-product of this town of marionettes — a broad, swaggering, grim, threateningly sedate fellow, with a jowl as large as a harvested wheat field, the complexion of a baptized infant and the knuckles of a prize-fighter. This type

leaned against cigar signs and viewed the world with
frappéd contumely.

A poet is a sensitive creature, and Raggles soon
shrivelled in the bleak embrace of the undecipherable.
The chill, sphynx-like, ironical, illegible, unnatural,
ruthless expression of the city left him downcast and
bewildered. Had it no heart? Better the woodpile,
the scolding of vinegar-faced housewives at back doors,
the kindly spleen of bartenders behind provincial free-
lunch counters, the amiable truculence of rural con-
stables, the kicks, arrests and happy-go-lucky chances
of the other vulgar, loud, crude cities than this freez-
ing heartlessness.

Raggles summoned his courage and sought alms
from the populace. Unheeding, regardless, they
passed on without the wink of an eyelash to testify
that they were conscious of his existence. And then
he said to himself that this fair but pitiless city of
Manhattan was without a soul; that its inhabitants
were manikins moved by wires and springs, and that
he was alone in a great wilderness.

Raggles started to cross the street. There was a
blast, a roar, a hissing and a crash as something
struck him and hurled him over and over six yards
from where he had been. As he was coming down like
the stick of a rocket the earth and all the cities thereof
turned to a fractured dream.

Raggles opened his eyes. First an odor made it-

[108]

self known to him — an odor of the earliest spring flowers of Paradise. And then a hand soft as a falling petal touched his brow. Bending over him was the woman clothed like the princess of old, with blue eyes, now soft and humid with human sympathy. Under his head on the pavement were silks and furs. With Raggles's hat in his hand and with his face pinker than ever from a vehement burst of oratory against reckless driving, stood the elderly gentleman who personified the city's wealth and ripeness. From a nearby café hurried the by-product with the vast jowl and baby complexion, bearing a glass full of a crimson fluid that suggested delightful possibilities.

"Drink dis, sport," said the by-product, holding the glass to Raggles's lips.

Hundreds of people huddled around in a moment, their faces wearing the deepest concern. Two flattering and gorgeous policemen got into the circle and pressed back the overplus of Samaritans. An old lady in a black shawl spoke loudly of camphor; a newsboy slipped one of his papers beneath Raggles's elbow, where it lay on the muddy pavement. A brisk young man with a notebook was asking for names.

A bell clanged importantly, and the ambulance cleaned a lane through the crowd. A cool surgeon slipped into the midst of affairs.

"How do you feel, old man?" asked the surgeon, stooping easily to his task. The princess of silks and

[109]

satins wiped a red drop or two from Raggles's brow
with a fragrant cobweb.

" Me? " said Raggles, with a seraphic smile, " I
feel fine."

He had found the heart of his new city.

In three days they let him leave his cot for the
convalescent ward in the hospital. He had been in
there an hour when the attendants hear sounds of
conflict. Upon investigation they found that Raggles
had assaulted and damaged a brother convalescent —
a glowering transient whom a freight train collision
had sent in to be patched up.

" What's all this about? " inquired the head nurse.

" He was runnin' down me town," said Raggles.

" What town? " asked the nurse.

" Noo York," said Raggles.

VANITY AND SOME SABLES

WHEN "Kid" Brady was sent to the ropes by Molly McKeever's blue-black eyes he withdrew from the Stovepipe Gang. So much for the power of a colleen's blanderin' tongue and stubborn true-heartedness. If you are a man who read this, may such an influence be sent you before 2 o'clock to-morrow; if you are a woman, may your Pomeranian greet you this morning with a cold nose — a sign of doghealth and your happiness.

The Stovepipe Gang borrowed its name from a sub-district of the city called the "Stovepipe," which is a narrow and natural extension of the familiar district known as "Hell's Kitchen." The "Stovepipe" strip of town runs along Eleventh and Twelfth avenues on the river, and bends a hard and sooty elbow around little, lost homeless DeWitt Clinton park. Consider that a stovepipe in an important factor in any kitchen and the situation is analyzed. The chefs in "Hell's Kitchen" are many, and the "Stovepipe" gang wears the cordon blue.

The members of this uncharted but widely known brotherhood appeared to pass their time on street corners arrayed like the lilies of the conservatory and

[111]

busy with nail files and penknives. Thus displayed as a guarantee of good faith, they carried on an innocuous conversation in a 200-word vocabulary, to the casual observer as innocent and immaterial as that heard in the clubs seven blocks to the east.

But off exhibition the " Stovepipes " were not mere street corner ornaments addicted to posing and manicuring. Their serious occupation was the separating of citizens from their coin and valuables. Preferably this was done by wierd and singular tricks without noise or bloodshed; but whenever the citizen honored by their attentions refused to impoverish himself gracefully his objections came to be spread finally upon some police station blotter or hospital register.

The police held the " Stovepipe " gang in perpetual suspicion and respect. As the nightingale's liquid note is heard in the deepest shadows so along 'he " Stovepipe's " dark and narrow confines the whistle for reserves punctures the dull ear of night. Whenever there was smoke in the " Stovepipe " the tasselled men in blue knew there was fire in " Hell's Kitchen."

" Kid " Brady promised Molly to be good. " Kid " was the vainest, the strongest, the wariest and the most successful plotter in the gang. Therefore, the boys were sorry to give him up.

But they witnessed his fall to a virtuous life without protest. For, in the Kitchen it is considered neither unmanly nor improper for a guy to do as his girl advises.

Black her eye for love's sake, if you will; but it is all-to-the-good business to do a thing when she wants you to do it.

"Turn off the hydrant," said the Kid, one night when Molly, tearful, besought him to amend his ways. "I'm going to cut out the gang. You for mine, and the simple life on the side. I'll tell you, Moll — I'll get work; and in a year we'll get married. I'll do it for you. We'll get a flat and a flute, and a sewing machine and a rubber plant and live as honest as we can."

"Oh, Kid," sighed Molly, wiping the powder off his shoulder with her handkerchief, "I'd rather hear you say that than to own all of New York. And we can be happy on so little!"

The Kid looked down at his speckless cuffs and shining patent leathers with a suspicion of melancholy.

"It'll hurt hardest in the rags department," said he. "I've kind of always liked to rig out swell when I could. You know how I hate cheap things, Moll. This suit set me back sixty-five. Anything in the wearing apparel line has got to be just so, or it's to the misfit parlors for it, for mine. If I work I won't have so much coin to hand over to the little man with the big shears."

"Never mind, Kid. I'll like you just as much in a blue jumper as I would in a red automobile."

Before the Kid had grown large enough to knock out his father he had been compelled to learn the plumber's art. So now back to this honorable and useful profession he returned. But it was as an assistant that he engaged himself; and it is the master plumber and not the assistant, who wears diamonds as large as hailstones and looks contemptuously upon the marble colonades of Senator Clark's mansion.

Eight months went by as smoothly and surely as though they had "elapsed" on a theater program. The Kid worked away at his pipes and solder with no symptoms of backsliding. The Stovepipe gang continued its piracy on the high avenues, cracked policemen's heads, held up late travelers, invented new methods of peaceful plundering, copied Fifth avenue's cut of clothes and neckwear fancies and comported itself according to its lawless bylaws. But the Kid stood firm and faithful to his Molly, even though the polish was gone from his fingernails and it took him 15 minutes to tie his purple silk ascot so that the worn places would not show.

One evening he brought a mysterious bundle with him to Molly's house.

"Open that, Moll!" he said in his large, quiet way. "It's for you."

Molly's eager fingers tore off the wrappings. She

shrieked aloud, and in rushed a sprinkling of little McKeevers, and Ma McKeever, dishwashy, but an undeniable relative of the late Mrs. Eve.

Again Molly shrieked, and something dark and long and sinuous flew and enveloped her neck like an anaconda.

"Russian sables," said the Kid, pridefully, enjoying the sight of Molly's round cheek against the clinging fur. "The real thing. They don't grow anything in Russia too good for you, Moll."

Molly plunged her hands into the muff, overturned a row of the family infants and flew to the mirror. Hint for the beauty column. To make bright eyes, rosy cheeks and a bewitching smile: Recipe — one set Russian sables. Apply.

When they were alone Molly became aware of a small cake of the ice of common sense floating down the full tide of her happiness.

"You're a bird, all right, Kid," she admitted gratefully. "I never had any furs on before in my life. But ain't Russian sables awful expensive? Seems to me I've heard they were."

"Have I ever chucked any bargain-sale stuff at you, Moll?" asked the Kid, with calm dignity. "Did you ever notice me leaning on the remnant counter or peering in the window of the five-and-ten? Call that scarf $250 and the muff $175 and you won't make any mistake about the price of Russian sables.

The swell goods for me. Say, they look fine on you, Moll."

Molly hugged the sables to her bosom in rapture. And then her smile went away little by little, and she looked the Kid straight in the eye sadly and steadily.

He knew what every look of hers meant; and he laughed with a faint flush upon his face.

"Cut it out," he said, with affectionate roughness. "I told you I was done with that. I bought 'em and paid for 'em, all right, with my own money?"

"Out of the money you worked for, Kid? Out of $75 a month?"

"Sure. I been saving up."

"Let's see — saved $425 in eight months, Kid?"

"Ah, let up," said the Kid, with some heat. "I had some money when I went to work. Do you think I've been holding 'em up again? I told you I'd quit. They're paid for on the square. Put 'em on and come out for a walk."

Molly calmed her doubts. Sables are soothing. Proud as a queen she went forth in the streets at the Kid's side. In all that region of low-lying streets Russian sables had never been seen before. The word sped, and doors and windows blossomed with heads eager to see the swell furs Kid Brady had given his girl. All down the street there were " Oh's " and "Ah's," and the reported fabulous sum paid for the sables was passed from lip to lip, increasing as it went. At her right elbow sauntered the Kid with the air of princes. Work had not diminished his love of pomp and show and his passion for the costly and genuine. On a corner they saw a group of the Stovepipe Gang loafing, immaculate. They raised their hats to the Kid's girl and went on with their calm, unaccented palaver.

Three blocks behind the admired couple strolled Detective Ransom, of the Central office. Ransom was the only detective on the force who could walk abroad with safety in the Stovepipe district. He was fair dealing and unafraid and went there with the hypothesis that the inhabitants were human. Many liked him, and now and then one would tip off to him something that he was looking for.

"What's the excitement down the street?" asked Ransom of a pale youth in a red sweater.

"Dey're out rubberin' at a set of buffalo robes Kid Brady staked his girl to," answered the youth. "Some say he paid $900 for de skins. Dey're swell all right enough."

"I hear Brady has been working at his old trade for nearly a year," said the detective. "He doesn't travel with the gang any more, does he?"

"He's workin', all right," said the red sweater, "but —say, sport, are you trailin' anything in the fur line? A job in a plumbin' shop don't match wid dem skins de Kid's girl's got on."

Ransom overtook the strolling couple on an empty

street near the river bank. He touched the Kid's arm from behind.

"Let me see you a moment, Brady," he said, quietly. His eye rested for a second on the long fur scarf thrown stylishly back over Molly's left shoulder. The Kid, with his old-time police hating frown on his face, stepped a yard or two aside with the detecive.

"Did you go to Mrs. Hethcote's on West 7—th street yesterday to fix a leaky water pipe?" asked Ransom.

"I did," said the Kid. "What of it?"

"The lady's $1,000 set of Russian sables went out of the house about the same time you did. The description fits the ones this lady has on."

"To h — Harlem with you," cried the Kid, angrily. "You know I've cut out that sort of thing, Ransom. I bought them sables yesterday at — "

The Kid stopped short.

"I know you've been working straight lately," said Ransom. "I'll give you every chance. I'll go with you where you say you bought the furs and investigate. The lady can wear 'em along with us and nobody'll be on. That's fair, Brady."

"Come on," agreed the Kid, hotly. And then he stopped suddenly in his tracks and looked with an odd smile at Molly's distressed and anxious face.

"No use," he said, grimly. "They're the Heth-

[118]

cote sables, all right. You'll have to turn 'em over, Moll, but they ain't too good for you if they cost a million."

Molly, with anguish in her face, hung upon the Kid's arm.

" Oh, Kiddy, you've broke my heart," she said. " I was so proud of you — and now they'll do you — and where's our happiness gone? "

" Go home," said the Kid, wildly. " Come on, Ransom — take the furs. Let's get away from here. Wait a minute — I've a good mind to — no, I'll be d — if I can do it — run along, Moll — I'm ready, Ransom."

Around the corner of a lumber-yard came Policeman Kohen on his way to his beat along the river. The detective signed to him for assistance. Kohen joined the group. Ransom explained.

" Sure," said Kohen. " I hear about those saples dat vas stole. You say you have dem here? "

Policeman Kohen took the end of Molly's late scarf in his hands and looked at it closely.

" Once," he said, " I sold furs in Sixth avenue. Yes, dese are saples. Dey come from Alaska. Dis scarf is vort $12 and dis muff — "

" Biff ! " came the palm of the Kid's powerful hand upon the policeman's mouth. Kohen staggered and rallied. Molly screamed. The detective threw him-

[119]

self upon Brady and with Kohen's aid got the nippers on his wrist.

" The scarf is vort $12 and the muff is vort $9," persisted the policeman. " Vot is dis talk about $1,000 saples? "

The Kid sat upon a pile of lumber and his face turned dark red.

" Correct, Solomonski! " he declared, viciously. " I paid $21.50 for the set. I'd rather have got six months and not have told it. Me, the swell guy that wouldn't look at anything cheap! I'm a plain bluffer. Moll — my salary couldn't spell sables in Russian."

Molly cast herself upon his neck.

" What do I care for all the sables and money in the world," she cried. " It's my Kiddy I want. Oh, you dear, stuck-up, crazy blockhead! "

" You can take dose nippers off," said Kohen to the detective. " Before I leaf de station de report come in dat de lady vind her saples — hanging in her wardrobe. Young man, I excuse you dat punch in my vace — dis von time."

Ransom handed Molly her furs. Her eyes were smiling upon the Kid. She wound the scarf and threw the end over her left shoulder with a duchess' grace.

" A gouple of young vools," said Policeman Kohen to Ransom: " come on away."

THE SOCIAL TRIANGLE

A T the stroke of six Ikey Snigglefritz laid down his
goose. Ikey was a tailor's apprentice. Are there
tailor's apprentices nowadays?

At any rate, Ikey toiled and snipped and basted
and pressed and patched and sponged all day in the
steamy fetor of a tailor-shop. But when work was
done Ikey hitched his wagon to such stars as his firma-
ment let shine.

It was Saturday night, and the boss laid twelve
begrimed and begrudged dollars in his hand. Ikey
dabbled discreetly in water, donned coat, hat and
collar with its frazzled tie and chalcedony pin, and
set forth in pursuit of his ideals.

For each of us, when our day's work is done, must
seek our ideal, whether it be love or pinochle or lobster á la Newburg, or the sweet silence of the musty
bookshelves.

Behold Ikey as he ambles up the street beneath the
roaring " El " between the rows of reeking sweat-
shops. Pallid, stooping, insignificant, squalid, doomed
to exist forever in penury of body and mind, yet,
as he swings his cheap cane and projects the noisome
inhalations from his cigarette, you perceive that he

nurtures in his narrow bosom the bacillus of society.

Ikey's legs carried him to and into that famous place of entertainment known as the Café Maginnis — famous because it was the rendezvous of Billy Mc-Mahan, the greatest man, the most wonderful man, Ikey thought, that the world had ever produced.

Billy McMahan was the district leader. Upon him the Tiger purred, and his hand held manna to scatter. Now, as Ikey entered, McMahan stood, flushed and triumphant and mighty, the centre of a huzzaing con-course of his lieutenants and constituents. It seems there had been an election; a signal victory had been won; the city had been swept back into line by a re-sistless besom of ballots.

Ikey slunk along the bar and gazed, breath-quick-ened, at his idol.

How magnificent was Billy McMahan, with his great, smooth, laughing face; his gray eye, shrewd as a chicken hawk's; his diamond ring, his voice like a bugle call, his prince's air, his plump and active roll of money, his clarion call to friend and comrade — oh, what a king of men he was! How he obscured his lieutenants, though they themselves loomed large and serious, blue of chin and important of mien, with hands buried deep in the pockets of their short over-coats! But Billy — oh, what small avail are words to paint for you his glory as seen by Ikey Snigglefritz!

The Café Maginnis rang to the note of victory. The white-coated bartenders threw themselves featfully upon bottle, cork and glass. From a score of clear Havanas the air received its paradox of clouds. The leal and the hopeful shook Billy McMahan's hand. And there was born suddenly in the worshipful soul of Ikey Snigglefritz an audacious, thrilling impulse.

He stepped forward into the little cleared space in which majesty moved, and held out his hand.

Billy McMahan grasped it unhesitatingly, shook it and smiled.

Made mad now by the gods who were about to destroy him, Ikey threw away his scabbard and charged upon Olympus.

" Have a drink with me, Billy," he said familiarly, " you and your friends? "

" Don't mind if I do, old man," said the great leader, " just to keep the ball rolling."

The last spark of Ikey's reason fled.

" Wine," he called to the bartender, waving a trembling hand.

The corks of three bottles were drawn; the champagne bubbled in the long row of glasses set upon the bar. Billy McMahan took his and nodded, with his beaming smile, at Ikey. The lieutenants and satellites took theirs and growled " Here's to you." Ikey took his nectar in delirium. All drank.

[123]

Ikey threw his week's wages in a crumpled roll upon the bar.

" C'rect," said the bartender, smoothing the twelve one-dollar notes. The crowd surged around Billy McMahan again. Some one was telling how Brannigan fixed 'em over in the Eleventh. Ikey leaned against the bar a while, and then went out.

He went down Hester street and up Chrystie, and down Delancey to where he lived. And there his women folk, a bibulous mother and three dingy sisters, pounced upon him for his wages. And at his confession they shrieked and objurgated him in the pithy rhetoric of the locality.

But even as they plucked at him and struck him Ikey remained in his ecstatic trance of joy. His head was in the clouds; the star was drawing his wagon. Compared with what he had achieved the loss of wages and the bray of women's tongues were slight affairs.

He had shaken the hand of Billy McMahan.

* * * * * *

Billy McMahan had a wife, and upon her visiting cards was engraved the name " Mrs. William Darragh McMahan." And there was a certain vexation attendant upon these cards; for, small as they were, there were houses in which they could not be inserted. Billy McMahan was a dictator in politics, a four-walled tower in business, a mogul, dreaded, loved and obeyed among his own people. He was growing rich; the daily papers had a dozen men on his trail to chronicle his every word of wisdom; he had been honored in caricature holding the Tiger cringing in leash.

But the heart of Billy was sometimes sore within him. There was a race of men from which he stood apart but that he viewed with the eye of Moses looking over into the promised land. He, too, had ideals, even as had Ikey Snigglefritz; and sometimes, hopeless of attaining them, his own solid success was as dust and ashes in his mouth. And Mrs. William Darragh McMahan wore a look of discontent upon her plump but pretty face, and the very rustle of her silks seemed a sigh.

There was a brave and conspicuous assemblage in the dinning salon of a noted hostelry where Fashion loves to display her charms. At one table sat Billy McMahan and his wife. Mostly silent they were, but the accessories they enjoyed little needed the indorsement of speech. Mrs. McMahan's diamonds were outshone by few in the room. The waiter bore the costliest brands of wine to their table. In evening dress, with an expression of gloom upon his smooth and massive countenance, you would look in vain for a more striking figure than Billy's

Four tables away sat alone a tall, slender man, about thirty, with thoughtful, melancholy eyes, a Van

Dyke beard and peculiarly white, thin hands. He was dining on filet mignon, dry toast and appollinaris. That man was Cortlandt Van Duyckink, a man worth eighty millions, who inherited and held a sacred seat in the exclusive inner circle of society.

Billy McMahan spoke to no one around him, because he knew no one. Van Duyckink kept his eyes on his plate because he knew that every eye present was hungry to catch his. He could bestow knighthood and prestige by a nod, and he was chary of creating a too extensive nobility.

And then Billy McMahan conceived and accomplished the most startling and audacious act of his life. He rose deliberately and walked over to Cortlandt Van Duyckink's table and held out his hand.

"Say, Mr. Van Duyckink," he said, "I've heard you was talking about starting some reforms among the poor people down in my district. I'm McMahan, you know. Say, now, if that's straight I'll do all I can to help you. And what I says goes in that neck of the woods, don't it? Oh, say, I rather guess it does."

Van Duyckink's rather sombre eyes lighted up. He rose to his lank height and grasped Billy McMahan's hand.

"Thank you, Mr. McMahan," he said, in his deep, serious tones. "I have been thinking of doing some work of that sort. I shall be glad of your assistance.

It pleases me to have become acquainted with you."

Billy walked back to his seat. His shoulder was tingling from the accolade bestowed by royalty. A hundred eyes were now turned upon him in envy and new admiration. Mrs. William Darragh McMahan trembled with ecstasy, so that her diamonds smote the eye almost with pain. And now it was apparent that at many tables there were those who suddenly remembered that they enjoyed Mr. McMahan's acquaintance. He saw smiles and bows about him. He became enveloped in the aura of dizzy greatness. His campaign coolness deserted him.

"Wine for that gang!" he commanded the waiter, pointing with his finger. "Wine over there. Wine to those three gents by that green bush. Tell 'em it's on me. D —— n it! Wine for everybody!"

The waiter ventured to whisper that it was perhaps inexpedient to carry out the order, in consideration of the dignity of the house and its custom.

"All right," said Billy, "if it's against the rules. I wonder if 'twould do to send my friend Van Duyckink a bottle. No? Well, it'll flow all right at the caffy to-night, just the same. It'll be rubber boots for anybody who comes in there any time up to 2 A. M."

Billy McMahan was happy.

He had shaken the hand of Cortlandt Van Duyckink.

* * *

The big pale-gray auto with its shining metal work looked out of place moving slowly among the push-carts and trash-heaps on the lower east side. So did Cortlandt Van Duyckink, with his aristocratic face and white, thin hands, as he steered carefully between the groups of ragged, scurrying youngsters in the streets. And so did Miss Constance Schuyler, with her dim, ascetic beauty, seated at his side.

"Oh, Cortlandt," she breathed, "isn't it sad that human beings have to live in such wretchedness and poverty? And you — how noble it is of you to think of them, to give your time and money to improve their condition!"

Van Duyckink turned his solemn eyes upon her.

"It is little," he said, sadly, "that I can do. The question is a large one, and belongs to society. But even individual effort is not thrown away. Look, Constance! On this street I have arranged to build soup kitchens, where no one who is hungry will be turned away. And down this other street are the old buildings that I shall cause to be torn down and there erect others in place of those death-traps of fire and disease."

Down Delancey slowly crept the pale-gray auto. Away from it toddled coveys of wondering, tangle-haired, barefooted, unwashed children. It stopped before a crazy brick structure, foul and awry.

Van Duyckink alighted to examine at a better per-

spective one of the leaning walls. Down the steps of
the building came a young man who seemed to epi-
tomize its degradation, squalor and infelicity — a nar-
row-chested, pale, unsavory young man, puffing at a
cigarette.

Obeying a sudden impulse, Van Duyckink stepped
out and warmly grasped the hand of what seemed to
him a living rebuke.

" I want to know you people," he said, sincerely.
" I am going to help you as much as I can. We shall
be friends."

As the auto crept carefully away Courtlandt Van
Duyckink felt an unaccustomed glow about his heart.
He was near to being a happy man.

He had shaken the hand of Ikey Snigglefritz.

THE PURPLE DRESS

WE are to consider the shade known as purple. It is a color justly in repute among the sons and daughters of man. Emperors claim it for their especial dye. Good fellows everywhere seek to bring their noses to the genial hue that follows the commingling of the red and blue. We say of princes that they are born to the purple; and no doubt they are, for the colic tinges their faces with the royal tint equally with the snub-nosed countenance of a woodchopper's brat. All women love it — when it is the fashion.

And now purple is being worn. You notice it on the streets. Of course other colors are quite stylish as well — in fact, I saw a lovely thing the other day in olive green albatross, with a triple-lapped flounce skirt trimmed with insert squares of silk, and a draped fichu of lace opening over a shirred vest and double puff sleeves with a lace band holding two gathered frills — but you see lots of purple too. Oh, yes, you do; just take a walk down Twenty-third street any afternoon.

Therefore Maida — the girl with the big brown eyes and cinnamon-colored hair in the Bee-Hive Store — said to Grace — the girl with the rhinestone brooch

[130]

and peppermint-pepsin flavor to her speech —" I'm
going to have a purple dress — a tailor-made purple
dress — for Thanksgiving."

"Oh, are you," said Grace, putting away some 7½
gloves into the 6¾ box. "Well, it's me for red.
You see more red on Fifth avenue. And the men all
seem to like it."

"I like purple best," said Maida. "And old
Schlegel has promised to make it for $8. It's going
to be lovely. I'm going to have a plaited skirt and
a blouse coat trimmed with a band of galloon under a
white cloth collar with two rows of —"

"Sly boots!" said Grace with an educated wink.

" — soutache braid over a surpliced white vest; and
a plaited basque and —"

"Sly boots — sly boots!" repeated Grace.

"—plaited gigot sleeves with a drawn velvet ribbon
over an inside cuff. What do you mean by saying
that?"

"You think Mr. Ramsay likes purple. I heard
him say yesterday he thought some of the dark shades
of red were stunning."

"I don't care," said Maida. "I prefer purple, and
them that don't like it can just take the other side
of the street."

Which suggests the thought that after all, the fol-
lowers of purple may be subject to slight delusions.
Danger is near when a maiden thinks she can wear

purple regardless of complexions and opinions; and when Emperors think their purple robes will wear forever.

Maida had saved $18 after eight months of economy; and this had bought the goods for the purple dress and paid Schlegel $4 on the making of it. On the day before Thanksgiving she would have just enough to pay the remaining $4. And then for a holiday in a new dress — can earth offer anything more enchanting?

Old Bachman, the proprietor of the Bee-Hive Store, always gave a Thanksgiving dinner to his employees. On every one of the subsequent 364 days, excusing Sundays, he would remind them of the joys of the past banquet and the hopes of the coming ones, thus inciting them to increased enthusiasm in work. The dinner was given in the store on one of the long tables in the middle of the room. They tacked wrapping paper over the front windows; and the turkeys and other good things were brought in the back way from the restaurant on the corner. You will perceive that the Bee-Hive was not a fashionable department store, with escalators and pompadours. It was almost small enough to be called an emporium; and you could actually go in there and get waited on and walk out again. And always at the Thanksgiving dinners Mr. Ramsay —

Oh, bother! I should have mentioned Mr. Ramsay

first of all. He is more important than purple or green, or even the red cranberry sauce.

Mr. Ramsay was the head clerk; and as far as I am concerned I am for him. He never pinched the girls' arms when he passed them in dark corners of the store; and when he told them stories when business was dull and the girls giggled and said: " Oh, pshaw!" it wasn't G. Bernard they meant at all. Besides being a gentleman, Mr. Ramsay was queer and original in other ways. He was a health crank, and believed that people should never eat anything that was good for them. He was violently opposed to anybody being comfortable, and coming in out of snow storms, or wearing overshoes, or taking medicine, or coddling themselves in any way. Every one of the ten girls in the store had little pork-chop-and-fried-onion dreams every night of becoming Mrs. Ramsay. For, next year old Bachman was going to take him in for a partner. And each one of them knew that if she should catch him she would knock those cranky health notions of his sky high before the wedding cake indigestion was over.

Mr. Ramsay was master of ceremonies at the dinners. Always they had two Italians in to play a violin and harp and had a little dance in the store.

And here were two dresses being conceived to charm Ramsay — one purple and the other red. Of course, the other eight girls were going to have dresses too, but they didn't count. Very likely they'd wear some shirt-waist-and-black-skirt-affairs — nothing as resplendent as purple or red.

Grace had saved her money, too. She was going to buy her dress ready-made. Oh, what's the use of bothering with a tailor — when you've got a figger its easy to get a fit — the ready-made are intended for a perfect figger — except I have to have 'em all taken in at the waist — the average figger is so large waisted.

The night before Thanksgiving came. Maida hurried home, keen and bright with the thoughts of the blessed morrow. Her thoughts were of purple, but they were white themselves — the joyous enthusiasm of the young for the pleasures that youth must have or wither. She knew purple would become her, and — for the thousandth time she tried to assure herself that it was purple Mr. Ramsey said he liked and not red. She was going home first to get the $4 wrapped in a piece of tissue paper in the bottom drawer of her dresser, and then she was going to pay Schlegel and take the dress home herself.

Grace lived in the same house. She occupied the hall room above Maida's.

At home Maida found clamor and confusion. The landlady's tongue clattering sourly in the halls like a churn dasher dabbling in buttermilk. And then Grace came down to her room crying with eyes as red as any dress.

"She says I've got to get out," said Grace. "The old beast. Because I owe her $4. "She's put my trunk in the hall and locked the door. I can't go any-where else. I haven't got a cent of money."

"You had some yesterday," said Maida.

"I paid it on my dress," said Grace. "I thought she'd wait till next week for the rent."

Sniffle, sniffle, sob, sniffle.

Out came — out it had to come — Maida's $4.

"You blessed darling," cried Grace, now a rain-bow instead of sunset. "I'll pay the mean old thing and then I'm going to try on my dress. I think it's heavenly. Come up and look at it. I'll pay the money back, a dollar a week — honest I will."

Thanksgiving.

The dinner was to be at noon. At a quarter to twelve Grace switched into Maida's room. Yes, she looked charming. Red was her color. Maida sat by the window in her old cheviot skirt and blue waist darning a st —. Oh, doing fancy work.

"Why, goodness me! ain't you dressed yet?" shrilled the red one. "How does it fit in the back? Don't you think these velvet tabs look awful swell? Why ain't you dressed, Maida?"

"My dress didn't get finished in time," said Maida. "I'm not going to the dinner."

" That's too bad. Why, I'm awful sorry Maida. Why don't you put on anything and come along — it's just the store folks, you know, and they won't mind."

" I was set on my purple," said Maida. " If I can't have it I won't go at all. Don't bother about me. Run along or you'll be late. You look awful nice in red."

At her window Maida sat through the long morning and past the time of the dinner at the store. In her mind she could hear the girls shrieking over a pull-bone, could hear old Bachman's roar over his own deeply-concealed jokes, could see the diamonds of fat Mrs. Bachman, who came to the store only on Thanksgiving days, could see Mr. Ramsey moving about alert, kindly, looking to the comfort of all.

At four in the afternoon, with an expressionless face and a lifeless air she slowly made her way to Schlegel's shop and told him she could not pay the $4 due on the dress.

" Gott! " cried Schlegel, angrily. " For what do you look so glum? Take him away. He is ready. Pay me some time. Haf I not seen you pass mine shop every day in two years? If I make clothes is it that I do not know how to read beoples because? You will pay me some time when you can. Take him away. He is made goot; and if you look bretty in him all right. So. Pay me when you can."

Maida breathed a millionth part of the thanks in her heart, and hurried away with her dress. As she left the shop a smart dash of rain struck upon her face. She smiled and did not feel it.

Ladies who shop in carriages, you do not understand. Girls whose wardrobes are charged to the old man's account, you cannot begin to comprehend — you could not understand why Maida did not feel the cold dash of the Thanksgiving rain.

At five o'clock she went out upon the street wearing her purple dress. The rain had increased, and it beat down upon her in a steady, wind-blown pour. People were scurrying home and to cars with close-held umbrellas and tight buttoned raincoats. Many of them turned their heads to marvel at this beautiful, serene, happy-eyed girl in the purple dress walking through the storm as though she were strolling in a garden under summer skies.

I say you do not understand it, ladies of the full purse and varied wardrobe. You do not know what it is to live with a perpetual longing for pretty things — to starve eight months in order to bring a purple dress and a holiday together. What difference if it rained, hailed, blew, snowed, cycloned?

Maida had no umbrella nor overshoes. She had her purple dress and she walked abroad. Let the elements do their worst. A starved heart must have one crumb during a year. The rain ran down and dripped from her fingers.

Some one turned a corner and blocked her way. She looked up into Mr. Ramsey's eyes, sparkling with admiration and interest.

"Why, Miss Maida," said he, "you look simply magnificent in your new dress. I was greatly disappointed not to see you at our dinner. And of all the girls I ever knew, you show the greatest sense and intelligence. There is nothing more healthful and invigorating than braving the weather as you are doing. May I walk with you?"

And Maida blushed and sneezed.

THE FOREIGN POLICY OF COMPANY 99

JOHN BYRNES, hose-cart driver of Engine Company No. 99, was afflicted with what his comrades called Japanitis.

Byrnes had a war map spread permanently upon a table in the second story of the engine-house, and he could explain to you at any hour of the day or night the exact positions, conditions and intentions of both the Russian and Japanese armies. He had little clusters of pins stuck in the map which represented the opposing forces, and these he moved about from day to day in conformity with the war news in the daily papers.

Whenever the Japs won a victory John Byrnes would shift his pins, and then he would execute a war dance of delight, and the other firemen would hear him yell: " Go it, you blamed little, sawed-off, huckleberry-eyed, monkey-faced hot tamales! Eat 'em up, you little sleight-o'-hand, bow-legged bull terriers — give 'em another of them Yalu looloos, and you'll eat rice in St. Petersburg. Talk about your Russians — say, wouldn't they give you a painsky when it comes to a scrapovitch? "

Not even on the fair island of Nippon was there a

more enthusiastic champion of the Mikado's men. Supporters of the Russian cause did well to keep clear of Engine-House No. 99.

Sometimes all thoughts of the Japs left John Byrnes's head. That was when the alarm of fire had sounded and he was strapped in his driver's seat on the swaying cart, guiding Erebus and Joe, the finest team in the whole department — according to the crew of 99.

Of all the codes adopted by man for regulating his actions toward his fellow-mortals, the greatest are these — the code of King Arthur's Knights of the Round Table, the Constitution of the United States and the unwritten rules of the New York Fire Department. The Round Table methods are no longer practicable since the invention of street cars and breach-of-promise suits, and our Constitution is being found more and more unconstitutional every day, so the code of our firemen must be considered in the lead, with the Golden Rule and Jeffries's new punch trying for place and show.

The Constitution says that one man is as good as another; but the Fire Department says he is better. This is a too generous theory, but the law will not allow itself to be construed otherwise. All of which comes perilously near to being a paradox, and commends itself to the attention of the S. P. C. A.

One of the transatlantic liners dumped out at Ellis

Island a lump of protozoa which was expected to evolve into an American citizen. A steward kicked him down the gangway, a doctor pounced upon his eyes like a raven, seeking for trachoma or ophthalmia; he was hustled ashore and ejected into the city in the name of Liberty — perhaps, theoretically, thus inoculating against kingocracy with a drop of its own virus. This hypodermic injection of Europeanism wandered happily into the veins of the city with the broad grin of a pleased child. It was not burdened with baggage, cares or ambitions. Its body was lithely built and clothed in a sort of foreign fustian; its face was brightly vacant, with a small, flat nose, and was mostly covered by a thick, ragged, curling beard like the coat of a spaniel. In the pocket of the imported Thing were a few coins — denarii — scudi — kopecks — pfennigs — pilasters — whatever the financial nomenclature of his unknown country may have been.

Prattling to himself, always broadly grinning, pleased by the roar and movement of the barbarous city into which the steamship cut-rates had shunted him, the alien strayed away from the sea, which he hated, as far as the district covered by Engine Company No. 99. Light as a cork, he was kept bobbing along by the human tide, the crudest atom in all the silt of the stream that emptied into the reservoir of Liberty.

[141]

While crossing Third avenue he slowed his steps, enchanted by the thunder of the elevated trains above him and the soothing crash of the wheels on the cobbles. And then there was a new, delightful chord in the uproar — the musical clanging of a gong and a great shining juggernaut belching fire and smoke, that people were hurrying to see.

This beautiful thing, entrancing to the eye, dashed past, and the protoplasmic immigrant stepped into the wake of it with his broad, enraptured, uncomprehending grin. And so stepping, stepped into the path of No. 99's flying hose-cart, with John Byrnes gripping, with arms of steel, the reins over the plunging backs of Erebus and Joe.

The unwritten constitutional code of the firemen has no exceptions or amendments. It is a simple thing — as simple as the rule of three. There was the heedless unit in the right of way; there was the hose-cart and the iron pillar of the elevated railroad.

John Byrnes swung all his weight and muscle on the left rein. The team and cart swerved that way and crashed like a torpedo into the pillar. The men on the cart went flying like skittles. The driver's strap burst, the pillar rang with the shock, and John Byrnes fell on the car track with a broken shoulder twenty feet away, while Erebus — beautiful, raven-black, best-loved Erebus — lay whickering in his harness with a broken leg.

[142]

In consideration for the feelings of Engine Company No. 99 the details will be lightly touched. The company does not like to be reminded of that day. There was a great crowd, and hurry calls were sent in; and while the ambulance gong was clearing the way the men of No. 99 hard the crack of the S. P. C. A. agent's pistol, and turned their heads away, not daring to look toward Erebus again.

When the firemen got back to the engine-house they found that one of them was dragging by the collar the cause of their desolation and grief. They set it in the middle of the floor and gathered grimly about it. Through its whiskers the calamitous object chattered effervescently and waved its hands.

" Sounds like a seidlitz powder," said Mike Dowling, disgustedly, " and it makes me sicker than one. Call that a man! — that hoss was worth a steamer full of such two-legged animals. It's a immigrant — that's what it is."

" Look at the doctor's chalk mark on its coat," said Reilly, the desk man. " It's just landed. It must be a kind of a Dago or a Hun or one of them Finns, I guess. That's the kind of truck that Europe unloads onto us."

" Think of a thing like that getting in the way, and laying John up in hospital and spoiling the best fire team in the city," groaned another fireman. " It ought to be taken down to the dock and drowned."

"Somebody go around and get Sloviski," suggested the engine driver, "and let's see what nation is responsible for this conglomeration of hair and head noises."

Sloviski kept a delicatessen store around the corner on Third avenue, and was reputed to be a linguist.

One of the men fetched him — a fat, cringing man, with a discursive eye and the odors of many kinds of meats upon him.

"Take a whirl at this importation with your jaw-breakers, Sloviski," requested Mike Dowling. "We can't quite figure out whether he's from the Hackensack bottoms or Hongkong-on-the-Ganges."

Sloviski addressed the stranger in several dialects, that ranged in rhythm and cadence from the sounds produced by a tonsilitis gargle to the opening of a can of tomatoes with a pair of scissors. The immigrant replied in accents resembling the uncorking of a bottle of ginger ale.

"I have you his name," reported Sloviski. "You shall not pronounce it. Writing of it in paper is better." They gave him paper, and he wrote. "Demetre Svangvsk."

"Looks like short hand," said the desk man.

"He speaks some language," continued the interpreter, wiping his forehead, "of Austria and mixed with a little Turkish. And, den, he have some Magyar words and a Polish or two, and many like the

Roumanian, but not without talk of one tribe in Bess-arabia. I do not him quite understand."

"Would you call him a Dago or a Polocker, or what?" asked Mike, frowning at the polyglot description.

"He is a "— answered Sloviski —" he is a — I dink he come from — I dink he is a fool," he concluded, impatient at his linguistic failure, "and if you pleases I will go back at mine delicatessen."

"Whatever he is, he's a bird," said Mike Dowling; "and you want to watch him fly."

Taking by the wing the alien fowl that had fluttered into the nest of Liberty, Mike led him to the door of the engine-house and bestowed upon him a kick hearty enough to convey the entire animus of Company 99. Demetre Svangvsk hustled away down the sidewalk, turning once to show his ineradicable grin to the aggrieved firemen.

In three weeks John Byrnes was back at his post from the hospital. With great gusto he proceeded to bring his war map up to date. "My money on the Japs every time," he declared. "Why, look at them Russians — they're nothing but wolves. Wipe 'em out, I say — and the little old jiu jitsu gang are just the cherry blossoms to do the trick, and don't you forget it!"

The second day after Byrne's reappearance came Demetre Svangvsk, the unidentified, to the engine-house, with a broader grin than ever. He managed to convey the idea that he wished to congratulate the hose-cart driver on his recovery and to apologize for having caused the accident. This he accomplished by so many extravagant gestures and explosive noises that the company was diverted for half an hour. Then they kicked him out again, and on the next day he came back grinning. How or where he lived no one knew. And then John Byrnes's nine-year-old son, Chris, who brought him convalescent delicacies from home to eat, took a fancy to Svangvsk, and they allowed him to loaf about the door of the engine-house occasionally.

One afternoon the big drab automobile of the Deputy Fire Commissioner buzzed up to the door of No. 99 and the Deputy stepped inside for an informal inspection. The men kicked Svangvsk out a little harder than usual and proudly escorted the Deputy around 99, in which everything shone like my lady's mirror.

The Deputy respected the sorrow of the company concerning the loss of Erebus, and he had come to promise it another mate for Joe that would do him credit. So they let Joe out of his stall and showed the Deputy how deserving he was of the finest mate that could be in horsedom.

While they were circling around Joe confabbing, Chris climbed into the Deputy's auto and threw the power full on. The men heard a monster puffing and a shriek from the lad, and sprang out too late. The big auto shot away, luckily taking a straight course down the street. The boy knew nothing of its machinery; he sat clutching the cushions and howling. With the power on nothing could have stopped that auto except a brick house, and there was nothing for Chris to gain by such a stoppage.

Demetre Svankvsk was just coming in again with a grin for another kick when Chris played his merry little prank. While the others sprang for the door Demetre sprang for Joe. He glided upon the horse's bare back like a snake and shouted something at him like the crack of a dozen whips. One of the firemen afterward swore that Joe answered him back in the same language. Ten seconds after the auto started the big horse was eating up the asphalt behind it like a strip of macaroni.

Some people two blocks and a half away saw the rescue. They said that the auto was nothing but a drab noise with a black speck in the middle of it for Chris, when a big bay horse with a lizard lying on its back cantered up alongside of it, and the lizard reached over and picked the black speck out of the noise.

Only fifteen minutes after Svangvsk's last kicking at the hands — or rather the feet — of Engine Company No. 99 he rode Joe back through the door with the boy safe, but acutely conscious of the licking he was going to receive.

Svangvsk slipped to the floor, leaned his head against Joe's and made a noise like a clucking hen. Joe nodded and whistled loudly through his nostrils, putting to shame the knowledge of Sloviski, of the delicatessen.

John Byrnes walked up to Svangvsk, who grinned, expecting to be kicked. Byrnes gripped the outlander so strongly by the hand that Demetre grinned anyhow, conceiving it to be a new form of punishment.

" The heathen rides like a Cossack," remarked a fireman who had seen a Wild West show —" they're the greatest riders in the world."

The word seemed to electrify Svankvsk. He grinned wider than ever.

" Yas — yas — me Cossack," he spluttered, striking his chest.

" Cossack ! " repeated John Byrnes, thoughtfully, " ain't that a kind of a Russian? "

" They're one of the Russian tribes, sure," said the desk man, who read books between fire alarms.

Just then Alderman Foley, who was on his way home and did not know of the runaway, stopped at the door of the engine-house and called to Byrnes:

" Hello there, Jimmy, me boy — how's the war coming along? Japs still got the bear on the trot, have they? "

" Oh, I don't know," said John Byrnes, argumentatively, " them Japs haven't got any walkover. You wait till Kuropatkin gets a good whack at 'em and they won't be knee-high to a puddle-ducksky."

THE LOST BLEND

SINCE the bar has been blessed by the clergy, and cocktails open the dinners of the elect, one may speak of the saloon. Teetotalers need not listen, if they choose; there is always the slot restaurant, where a dime dropped into the cold bouillon aperture will bring forth a dry Martini.

Con Lantry worked on the sober side of the bar in Kenealy's café. You and I stood, one-legged like geese, on the other side and went into voluntary liquidation with our week's wages. Opposite danced Con, clean, temperate, clear-headed, polite, white-jacketed, punctual, trustworthy, young, responsible, and took our money.

The saloon (whether blessed or cursed) stood in one of those little " places " which are parallelograms instead of streets, and inhabited by laundries, decayed Knickerbocker families and Bohemians who have nothing to do with either.

Over the café lived Kenealy and his family. His daughter Katherine had eyes of dark Irish — but why should you be told? Be content with your Geraldine or your Eliza Ann. For Con dreamed of her; and when she called softly at the foot of the back stairs

[150]

for the pitcher of beer for dinner, his heart went up
and down like a milk punch in the shaker. Orderly
and fit are the rules of Romance; and if you hurl the
last shilling of your fortune upon the bar for whiskey,
the bartender shall take it, and marry his boss's daughter, and good will grow out of it.

But not so Con. For in the presence of woman he
was tongue-tied and scarlet. He who would quell
with his eye the sonorous youth whom the claret punch
made loquacious, or smash with lemon squeezer the
obstreperous, or hurl gutterward the cantakerous without a wrinkle coming to his white lawn tie, when he
stood before woman he was voiceless, incoherent, stut-
tering, buried beneath a hot avalanche of bashfulness
and misery. What then was he before Katherine? A
trembler, with no word to say for himself, a stone without blarney, the dumbest lover that ever babbled of
the weather in the presence of his divinity.

There came to Kenealy's two sunburned men, Riley
and McQuirk. They had conference with Kenealy;
and then they took possession of a back room which
they filled with bottles and siphons and jugs and
druggist's measuring glasses. All the appurtenances
and liquids of a saloon were there, but they dispensed
no drinks. All day long the two sweltered in there,
pouring and mixing unknown brews and decoctions
from the liquors in their store. Riley had the educa-
tion, and he figured on reams of paper, reducing gal-

lons to ounces and quarts to fluid drams. McQuirk, a morose man with a red eye, dashed each unsuccessful completed mixture into the waste pipes with curses gentle, husky and deep. They labored heavily and untiringly to achieve some mysterious solution like two alchemists striving to resolve gold from the elements.

Into this back room one evening when his watch was done sauntered Con. His professional curiosity had been stirred by these occult bartenders at whose bar none drank, and who daily drew upon Kenealy's store of liquors to follow their consuming and fruitless experiments.

Down the back stairs came Katherine with her smile like sunrise on Gweebarra Bay.

"Good evening, Mr. Lantry," says she. "And what is the news to-day, if you please?"

"It looks like r-rain," stammered the shy one, backing to the wall.

"It couldn't do better," said Katherine. "I'm thinking there's nothing the worse off for a little water." In the back room Riley and McQuirk toiled like bearded witches over their strange compounds. From fifty bottles they drew liquids carefully measured after Riley's figures, and shook the whole together in a great glass vessel. Then McQuirk would dash it out, with gloomy profanity, and they would begin again.

"Sit down," said Riley to Con, "and I'll tell you.

THE LOST BLEND

"Last summer me and Tim concludes that an American bar in this nation of Nicaragua would pay. There was a town on the coast where there's nothing to eat but quinine and nothing to drink but rum. The natives and foreigners lay down with chills and get up with fevers; and a good mixed drink is nature's remedy for all such tropical inconveniences.

"So we lays in a fine stock of wet goods in New York, and bar fixtures and glassware, and we sails for that Santa Palma town on a lime steamer. On the way me and Tim sees flying fish and plays seven-up with the captain and steward, and already begins to feel like the high-ball kings of the tropic of Capricorn.

"When we gets in five hours of the country that we was going to introduce to long drinks and short change the captain calls us over to the starboard binnacle and recollects a few things.

"'I forgot to tell you, boys,' says he, 'that Nicaragua slapped an import duty of 48 per cent. ad valorem on all bottled goods last month. The President took a bottle of Cincinnati hair tonic by mistake for tabasco sauce, and he's getting even. Barrelled goods is free.'

"Sorry you didn't mention it sooner," says we. And we bought two forty-two gallon casks from the captain, and opened every bottle we had and dumped the stuff all together in the casks. That 48 per cent.

would have ruined us; so we took the chances on making that $1,200 cocktail rather than throw the stuff away.

"Well, when we landed we tapped one of the barrels. The mixture was something heartrending. It was the color of a plate of Bowery pea soup, and it tasted like one of those coffee substitutes your aunt makes you take for the heart trouble you get by picking losers. We gave a nigger four fingers of it to try it, and he lay under a cocoanut tree three days beating the sand with his heels and refused to sign a testimonial.

"But the other barrel! Say, bartender, did you ever put on a straw hat with a yellow band around it and go up in a balloon with a pretty girl with $8,000,000 in your pocket all at the same time? That's what thirty drops of it would make you feel like. With two fingers of it inside you you would bury your face in your hands and cry because there wasn't anything more worth while around for you to lick than little Jim Jeffries. Yes, sir, the stuff in that second barrel was distilled elixir of battle, money and high life. It was the color of gold and as clear as glass, and it shone after dark like the sunshine was still in it. A thousand years from now you'll get a drink like that across the bar.

"Well, we started up business with that one line of drinks, and it was enough. The piebald gentry of

[154]

that country stuck to it like a hive of bees. If that barrel had lasted that country would have become the greatest on earth. When we opened up of mornings we had a line of Generals and Colonels and ex-Presidents and revolutionists a block long waiting to be served. We started in at 50 cents silver a drink. The last ten gallons went easy at $5 a gulp. It was wonderful stuff. It gave a man courage and ambition and nerve to do anything; at the same time he didn't care whether his money was tainted or fresh from the Ice Trust. When that barrel was half gone Nicaragua had repudiated the National debt, removed the duty on cigarettes and was about to declare war on the United States and England.

"'Twas by accident we discovered this king of drinks, and 'twill be by good luck if we strike it again. For ten months we've been trying. Small lots at a time, we've mixed barrels of all the harmful ingredients known to the profession of drinking. Ye could have stocked ten bars with the whiskeys, brandies, cordials, bitters, gins and wines me and Tim have wasted. A glorious drink like that to be denied to the world! 'Tis a sorrow and a loss of money. The United States as a nation would welcome a drink of the sort, and pay for it."

All the while McQuirk had been carefully measuring and pouring together small quantities of various spirits, as Riley called them, from his latest pencilled prescription. The completed mixture was of a vile, mottled chocolate color. McQuirk tasted it, and hurled it, with appropriate epithets, into the waste sink.

" 'Tis a strange story, even if true," said Con. " I'll be going now along to my supper."

" Take a drink," said Riley. " We've all kinds except the lost blend."

" I never drink," said Con, " anything stronger than water. I am just after meeting Miss Katherine by the stairs. She said a true word. ' There's not anything,' says she, ' but is better off for a little water.' "

When Con had left them Riley almost felled McQuirk by a blow on the back.

" Did ye hear that? " he shouted. " Two fools are we. The six dozen bottles of 'pollinaris we had on the ship — ye opened them yourself — which barrel did ye pour them in — which barrel, ye mudhead? "

" I mind," said McQuirk, slowly, " 'twas in the second barrel we opened. I mind the blue piece of paper pasted on the side of it."

" We've got it now," cried Riley. " 'Twas that we lacked. 'Tis the water that does the trick. Everything else we had right. Hurry, man, and get two bottles of 'pollinaris from the bar, while I figure out the proportionments with me pencil."

An hour later Con strolled down the sidewalk toward Kenealy's cafe. Thus faithful employees haunt,

during their recreation hours, the vicinity where they
labor, drawn by some mysterious attraction.

A police patrol wagon stood at the side door.
Three able cops were half carrying, half hustling
Riley and McQuirk up its rear steps. The eyes and
faces of each bore the bruises and cuts of sanguinary
and assiduous conflict. Yet they whooped with
strange joy, and directed upon the police the feeble
remnants of their pugnacious madness.

"Began fighting each other in the back room," explained Kenealy to Con. "And singing! That was
worse. Smashed everything pretty much up. But
they're good men. They'll pay for everything.
Trying to invent some new kind of cocktail, they was.
I'll see they come out all right in the morning."

Con sauntered into the back room to view the battlefield. As he went through the hall Katherine was just
coming down the stairs.

"Good evening again, Mr. Lantry," said she.
"And is there no news from the weather yet?"

"Still threatens r-rain," said Con slipping past with
red in his smooth, pale cheek.

Riley and McQuirk had indeed waged a great and
friendly battle. Broken bottles and glasses were
everywhere. The room was full of alcohol fumes; the
floor was variegated with spirituous puddles.

On the table stood a 32-ounce glass graduated
measure. In the bottom of it were two tablespoonfuls

of liquid — a bright golden liquid that seemed to hold the sunshine a prisoner in its auriferous depths.

Con smelled it. He tasted it. He drank it.

As he returned through the hall Katherine was just going up the stairs.

" No news yet, Mr. Lantry? " she asked with her teasing laugh.

Con lifted her clear from the floor and held her there.

" The news is," he said, " that we're to be married."

" Put me down, sir! " she cried indignantly, " or I will — Oh, Con, where, oh, wherever did you get the nerve to say it? "

A HARLEM TRAGEDY

HARLEM.

Mrs. Fink has dropped into Mrs. Cassidy's flat one flight below.

"Ain't it a beaut?" said Mrs. Cassidy.

She turned her face proudly for her friend Mrs. Fink to see. One eye was nearly closed, with a great, greenish-purple bruise around it. Her lip was cut and bleeding a little and there were red finger-marks on each side of her neck.

"My husband wouldn't ever think of doing that to me," said Mrs. Fink, concealing her envy.

"I wouldn't have a man," declared Mrs. Cassidy, "that didn't beat me up at least once a week. Shows he thinks something of you. Say! but that last dose Jack gave me wasn't no homeopathic one. I can see stars yet. But he'll be the sweetest man in town for the rest of the week to make up for it. This eye is good for theater tickets and a silk shirt waist at the very least."

"I should hope," said Mrs. Fink, assuming complacency, "that Mr. Fink is too much of a gentleman ever to raise his hand against me."

"Oh, go on, Maggie!" said Mrs. Cassidy, laughing

and applying witch hazel, " you're only jealous. Your old man is too frappéd and slow to ever give you a punch. He just sits down and practises physical culture with a newspaper when he comes home — now ain't that the truth? "

" Mr. Fink certainly peruses of the papers when he comes home," acknowledged Mrs. Fink, with a toss of her head; " but he certainly don't ever make no Steve O'Donnell out of me just to amuse himself — that's a sure thing."

Mrs. Cassidy laughed the contented laugh of the guarded and happy matron. With the air of Cornelia exhibiting her jewels, she drew down the collar of her kimono and revealed another treasured bruise, maroon-colored, edged with olive and orange — a bruise now nearly well, but still to memory dear.

Mrs. Fink capitulated. The formal light in her eye softened to envious admiration. She and Mrs. Cassidy had been chums in the downtown paper-box factory before they had married, one year before. Now she and her man occupied the flat above Mame and her man. Therefore she could not put on airs with Mame.

" Don't it hurt when he soaks you? " asked Mrs. Fink, curiously.

" Hurt ! "— Mrs. Cassidy gave a soprano scream of delight. " Well, say — did you ever have a brick house fall on you? — well, that's just the way it feels

— just like when they're digging you out of the ruins. Jack's got a left that spells two matinees and a new pair of Oxfords — and his right! — well, it takes a trip to Coney and six pairs of openwork, silk lisle threads to make that good."

"But what does he beat you for?" inquired Mrs. Fink, with wide-open eyes.

"Silly!" said Mrs. Cassidy, indulgently. "Why, because he's full. It's generally on Saturday nights."

"But what cause do you give him?" persisted the seeker after knowledge.

"Why, didn't I marry him? Jack comes in tanked up; and I'm here, ain't I? Who else has he got a right to beat? I'd just like to catch him once beating anybody else! Sometimes it's because supper ain't ready; and sometimes it's because it is. Jack ain't particular about causes. He just lushes till he remembers he's married, and then he makes for home and does me up. Saturday nights I just move the furniture with sharp corners out of the way, so I won't cut my head when he gets his work in. He's got a left swing that jars you! Sometimes I take the count in the first round; but when I feel like having a good time during the week or want some new rags I come up again for more punishment. That's what I done last night. Jack knows I've been wanting a black silk waist for a month, and I didn't think just one black eye would bring it. Tell you what, Mag, I'll bet you the ice cream he brings it to-night."

Mrs. Fink was thinking deeply.

" My Mart," she said, " never hit me a lick in his life. It's just like you said, Mame; he comes in grouchy and ain't got a word to say. He never takes me out anywhere. He's a chair-warmer at home for fair. He buys me things, but he looks so glum about it that I never appreciate 'em."

Mrs. Cassidy slipped an arm around her chum.

" You poor thing! " she said. " But everybody can't have a husband like Jack. Marriage wouldn't be no failure if they was all like him. These discontented wives you hear about — what they need is a man to come home and kick their slats in once a week, and then make it up in kisses, and chocolate creams. That'd give 'em some interest in life. What I want is a masterful man that slugs you when he's jagged and hugs you when he ain't jagged. Preserve me from the man that ain't got the sand to do neither! "

Mrs. Fink sighed.

The hallways were suddenly filled with sound. The door flew open at the kick of Mr. Cassidy. His arms were occupied with bundles. Mame flew and hung about his neck. Her sound eye sparkled with the love light that shines in the eye of the Maori maid when she recovers consciousness in the hut of the wooer who has stunned and dragged her there.

"Hello, old girl!" shouted Mr. Cassidy. He shed his bundles and lifted her off her feet in a mighty hug. "I got tickets for Barnum & Bailey's, and if you'll bust the string of one of them bundles I guess you'll find that silk waist — why, good evening, Mrs. Fink — I didn't see you at first. How's old Mart coming along?"

"He's very well, Mr. Cassidy — thanks," said Mrs. Fink. "I must be going along up now. Mart'll be home for supper soon. I'll bring you down that pattern you wanted to-morrow, Mame."

Mrs. Fink went up to her flat and had a little cry. It was a meaningless cry, the kind of cry that only a woman knows about, a cry from no particular cause, altogether an absurd cry; the most transient and the most hopeless cry in the repertory of grief. Why had Martin never thrashed her? He was as big and strong as Jack Cassidy. Did he not care for her at all? He never quarrelled; he came home and lounged about, silent, glum, idle. He was a fairly good provider, but he ignored the spices of life.

Mrs. Fink's ship of dreams was becalmed. Her captain ranged between plum duff and his hammock. If only he would shiver his timbers or stamp his foot on the quarter-deck now and then! And she had thought to sail so merrily, touching at ports in the Delectable Isles! But now, to vary the figure, she was ready to throw up the sponge, tired out, without a scratch to show for all those tame rounds with her sparring partner. For one moment she almost hated Mame — Mame, with her cuts and bruises, her salve of presents and kisses, her stormy voyage with her fighting, brutal, loving mate.

Mr. Fink came home at 7. He was permeated with the curse of domesticity. Beyond the portals of his cozy home he cared not to roam, to roam. He was the man who had caught the street car, the anaconda that had swallowed its prey, the tree that lay as it had fallen.

"Like the supper, Mart?" asked Mrs. Fink, who had striven over it.

"M-m-m-yep," grunted Mr. Fink.

After supper he gathered his newspapers to read. He sat in his stockinged feet.

Arise, some new Dante, and sing me the befitting corner of perdition for the man who sitteth in the house in his stockinged feet! Sisters of Patience who by reason of ties or duty have endured it in silk, yarn, cotton, lisle thread or woollen — does not the new canto belong?

The next day was Labor Day. The occupations of Mr. Cassidy and Mr. Fink ceased for one passage of the sun. Labor, triumphant, would parade and otherwise disport itself.

Mrs. Fink took Mrs. Cassidy's pattern down early. Mame had on her new silk waist. Even her damaged eye managed to emit a holiday gleam. Jack was fruitfully penitent, and there was a hilarious scheme for the day afoot, with parks and picnics and Pilsener in it.

A rising, indignant jealousy seized Mrs. Fink as she returned to her flat above. Oh, happy Mame, with her bruises and her quick-following balm! But was Mame to have a monopoly of happiness? Surely Martin Fink was as good a man as Jack Cassidy. Was his wife to go always unbelabored and uncaressed? A sudden, brilliant, breathless idea came to Mrs. Fink. She would show Mame that there were husbands as able to use their fists and perhaps to be as tender afterward as any Jack.

The holiday promised to be a nominal one with the Finks. Mrs. Fink had the stationary washtubs in the kitchen filled with a two weeks' wash that had been soaking overnight. Mr. Fink sat in his stockinged feet reading a newspaper. Thus Labor Day presaged to speed.

Jealousy surged high in Mrs. Fink's heart, and higher still surged an audacious resolve. If her man would not strike her — if he would not so far prove his manhood, his prerogative and his interest in conjugal affairs, he must be prompted to his duty.

Mr. Fink lit his pipe and peacefully rubbed an ankle with a stockinged toe. He reposed in the state of matrimony like a lump of unblended suet in a pudding. This was his level Elysium — to sit at ease vicariously girdling the world in print amid the wifely splashing of suds and the agreeable smells of breakfast dishes departed and dinner ones to come. Many ideas were far from his mind; but the furthest one was the thought of beating his wife.

Mrs. Fink turned on the hot water and set the washboards in the suds. Up from the flat below came the gay laugh of Mrs. Cassidy. It sounded like a taunt, a flaunting of her own happiness in the face of the unslugged bride above. Now was Mrs. Fink's time.

Suddenly she turned like a fury upon the man reading.

" You lazy loafer! " she cried, " must I work my arms off washing and toiling for the ugly likes of you? Are you a man or are you a kitchen hound? "

Mr. Fink dropped his paper, motionless from surprise. She feared that he would not strike — that the provocation had been insufficient. She leaped at him and struck him fiercely in the face with her clinched hand. In that instant she felt a thrill of love for him such as she had not felt for many a day. Rise up, Martin Fink, and come into your kingdom! Oh, she must feel the weight of his hand now — just to show that he cared — just to show that he cared!

Mr. Fink sprang to his feet — Maggie caught him again on the jaw with a wide swing of her other

[166]

hand. She closed her eyes in that fearful, blissful moment before his blow should come — she whispered his name to herself — she leaned to the expected shock, hungry for it.

In the flat below Mr. Cassidy, with a shamed and contrite face was powdering Mame's eye in preparation for their junket. From the flat above came the sound of a woman's voice, high-raised, a bumping, a stumbling and a shuffling, a chair overturned — unmistakable sounds of domestic conflict.

" Mart and Mag scrapping? " postulated Mr. Cassidy. " Didn't know they ever indulged. Shall I trot up and see if they need a sponge holder? "

One of Mrs. Cassidy's eyes sparkled like a diamond. The other twinkled at least like paste.

" Oh, oh," she said, softly and without apparent meaning, in the feminine ejaculatory manner. " I wonder if — I wonder if ! Wait, Jack, till I go up and see."

Up the stairs she sped. As her foot struck the hallway above out from the kitchen door of her flat wildly flounced Mrs. Fink.

" Oh, Maggie," cried Mrs. Cassidy, in a delighted whisper; " did he? Oh, did he? "

Mrs. Fink ran and laid her face upon her chum's shoulder and sobbed hopelessly.

Mrs. Cassidy took Maggie's face between her hands and lifted it gently. Tear-stained it was, flushing and paling, but its velvety, pink-and-white, becomingly freckled surface was unscratched, unbruised, unmarred by the recreant fist of Mr. Fink.

" Tell me, Maggie," pleaded Mame, " or I'll go in there and find out. What was it? Did he hurt you — what did he do? "

Mrs. Fink's face went down again despairingly on the bosom of her friend.

" For Gawd's sake don't open that door, Mame," she sobbed. " And don't ever tell nobody — keep it under your hat. He — he never touched me, and — he's — oh, Gawd — he's washin' the clothes — he's washin' the clothes! "

"THE GUILTY PARTY"

A RED-HAIRED, unshaven, untidy man sat in a rocking-chair by a window. He had just lighted a pipe, and was puffing blue clouds with great satisfaction. He had removed his shoes and donned a pair of blue, faded carpet-slippers. With the morbid thirst of the confirmed daily news drinker, he awkwardly folded back the pages of an evening paper, eagerly gulping down the strong, black headlines, to be followed as a chaser by the milder details of the smaller type.

In an adjoining room a woman was cooking supper. Odors from strong bacon and boiling coffee contended against the cut-plug fumes from the vespertine pipe.

Outside was one of those crowded streets of the east side, in which, as twilight falls, Satan sets up his recruiting office. A mighty host of children danced and ran and played in the street. Some in rags, some in clean white and beribboned, some wild and restless as young hawks, some gentle-faced and shrinking, some shrieking rude and sinful words, some listening, awed, but soon, grown familiar, to embrace — here were the children playing in the corridors of the House of Sin. Above the playground forever hovered a great bird. The bird was known to humorists as the stork. But the people of Chrystie street were better ornithologists. They called it a vulture.

A little girl of twelve came up timidly to the man reading and resting by the window, and said:

"Papa, won't you play a game of checkers with me if you aren't too tired?"

The red-haired, unshaven, untidy man sitting shoeless by the window answered, with a frown:

"Checkers! No, I won't. Can't a man who works hard all day have a little rest when he comes home? Why don't you go out and play with the other kids on the sidewalk?"

The woman who was cooking came to the door.

"John," she said, "I don't like for Lizzie to play in the street. They learn too much there that ain't good for 'em. She's been in the house all day long. It seems that you might give up a little of your time to amuse her when you come home."

"Let her go out and play like the rest of 'em if she wants to be amused," said the red-haired, unshaven, untidy man, "and don't bother me."

* * *

"You're on," said Kid Mullaly. "Fifty dollars to $25 I take Annie to the dance. Put up."

The Kid's black eyes were snapping with the fire

[170]

of the baited and challenged. He drew out his
" roll " and slapped five tens upon the bar. The
three or four young fellows who were thus " taken "
more slowly produced their stake. The bartender, ex-
officio stakeholder, took the money, laboriously
wrapped it, recorded the bet with an inch-long pencil
and stuffed the whole into a corner of the cash register.

" And, oh, what'll be done to you'll be a plenty,"
said a bettor, with anticipatory glee.

" That's my lookout," said the " Kid," sternly.
" Fill 'em up all around, Mike."

After the round Burke, the " Kid's " sponge,
sponge-holder, pal, Mentor and Grand Vizier, drew
him out to the bootblack stand at the saloon corner,
where all the official and important matters of the
Small Hours Social Club were settled. As Tony polished the light tan shoes of the club's President and
Secretary for the fifth time that day, Burke spake
words of wisdom to his chief.

" Cut that blond out, ' Kid,' " was his advice, " or
there'll be trouble. What do you want to throw down
that girl of yours for? You'll never find one that'll
freeze to you like Liz has. She's worth a hallful of
Annies."

" I'm no Annie admirer! " said the " Kid," dropping a cigarette ash on his polished toe, and wiping
it off on Tony's shoulder. " But I want to teach Liz

[171]

a lesson. She thinks I belong to her. She's been bragging that I daren't speak to another girl. Liz is all right — in some ways. She's drinking a little too much lately. And she uses language that a lady oughtn't."

"You're engaged, ain't you?" asked Burke.

"Sure. We'll get married next year, maybe."

"I saw you make her drink her first glass of beer," said Burke. "That was two years ago, when she used to come down to the corner of Chrystie bareheaded to meet you after supper. She was a quiet sort of a kid then, and couldn't speak without blushing."

"She's a little spitfire, sometimes, now," said the Kid. "I hate jealousy. That's why I'm going to the dance with Annie. It'll teach her some sense."

"Well, you better look a little out," were Burke's last words. "If Liz was my girl and I was to sneak out to a dance coupled up with an Annie, I'd want a suit of chain armor on under my gladsome rags, all right."

Through the land of the stork-vulture wandered Liz. Her black eyes searched the passing crowds fierily but vaguely. Now and then she hummed bars of foolish little songs. Between times she set her small, white teeth together, and spake crisp words that the east side has added to language.

Liz's skirt was green silk. Her waist was a large

brown-and-pink plaid, well-fitting and not without style. She wore a cluster ring of huge imitation rubies, and a locket that banged her knees at the bottom of a silver chain. Her shoes were run down over twisted high heels, and were strangers to polish. Her hat would scarcely have passed into a flour barrel.

The "Family Entrance" of the Blue Jay Café received her. At a table she sat, and punched the button with the air of milady ringing for her carriage. The waiter came with his large chinned, low-voiced manner of respectful familiarity. Liz smoothed her silken skirt with a satisfied wriggle. She made the most of it. Here she could order and be waited upon. It was all that her world offered her of the prerogative of woman.

"Whiskey, Tommy," she said as her sisters further uptown murmur, "Champagne, James."

"Sure, Miss Lizzie. What'll the chaser be?"

"Seltzer. And say, Tommy, has the Kid been around to-day?"

"Why, no, Miss Lizzie, I haven't saw him to-day."

Fluently came the "Miss Lizzie," for the Kid was known to be one who required rigid upholdment of the dignity of his fiancee.

"I'm lookin' for 'm," said Liz, after the chaser had sputtered under her nose. "It's got to me that he says he'll take Annie Karlson to the dance. Let him. The pink-eyed white rat! I'm lookin' for 'm. You know me, Tommy. Two years me and the Kid've been engaged. Look at that ring. Five hundred, he said it cost. Let him take her to the dance. What'll I do? I'll cut his heart out. Another whiskey, Tommy."

" I wouldn't listen to no such reports, Miss Lizzie," said the waiter smoothly, from the narrow opening above his chin. " Kid Mullaly's not the guy to throw a lady like you down. Seltzer on the side? "

" Two years," repeated Liz, softening a little to sentiment under the magic of the distiller's art. " I always used to play out on the street of evenin's 'cause there was nothin' doin' for me at home. For a long time I just sat on doorsteps and looked at the lights and the people goin' by. And then the Kid came along one evenin' and sized me up, and I was mashed on the spot for fair. The first drink he made me take I cried all night at home, and got a lickin' for makin' a noise. And now — say, Tommy, you ever see this Annie Karlson? If it wasn't for peroxide the chloroform limit would have put her out long ago. Oh, I'm lookin' for 'm. You tell the Kid if he comes in. Me? I'll cut his heart out. Leave it to me. Another whiskey, Tommy."

A little unsteadily, but with watchful and brilliant eyes, Liz walked up the avenue. On the doorstep of a brick tenement a curly-haired child sat, puzzling over the convolutions of a tangled string. Liz flopped down beside her, with a crooked, shifting smile on her flushed face. But her eyes had grown clear and artless of a sudden.

" Let me show you how to make a cats-cradle, kid," she said, tucking her green silk skirt under her rusty shoes.

And while they sat there the lights were being turned on for the dance in the hall of the Small Hours Social Club. It was the bi-monthly dance, a dress affair in which the members took great pride and bestirred themselves huskily to further and adorn.

At 9 o'clock the President, Kid Mullaly, paced upon the floor with a lady on his arm. As the Loreley's was her hair golden. Her " yes " was softened to a " yah," but its quality of assent was patent to the most Milesian ears. She stepped upon her own train and blushed, and — she smiled into the eyes of Kid Mullaly.

And then, as the two stood in the middle of the waxed floor, the thing happened to prevent which many lamps are burning nightly in many studies and libraries.

Out from the circle of spectators in the hall leaped Fate in a green silk skirt, under the *nom de guerre* of " Liz." Her eyes were hard and blacker than jet. She did not scream or waver. Most unwomanly, she cried out one oath — the Kid's own favorite oath — and in his own deep voice; and then while the Small Hours Social Club went frantically to pieces, she made good her boast to Tommy, the waiter — made good as far as the length of her knife blade and the strength of her arm permitted.

And next came the primal instinct of self-preservation — or was it self-annihilation, the instinct that society has grafted on the natural branch?

Liz ran out and down the street swift and true as a woodcock flying through a grove of saplings at dusk.

And then followed the big city's biggest shame, its most ancient and rotten surviving canker, its pollution and disgrace, its blight and perversion, its forever infamy and guilt, fostered, unreproved and cherished, handed down from a long-ago century of the basest barbarity — the Hue and Cry. Nowhere but in the big cities does it survive, and here most of all, where the ultimate perfection of culture, citizenship and alleged superiority joins, bawling, in the chase.

They pursued — a shrieking mob of fathers, mothers, lovers and maidens — howling, yelling, calling, whistling, crying for blood. Well may the wolf in the big city stand outside the door. Well may his heart, the gentler, falter at the siege.

Knowing her way, and hungry for her surcease, she darted down the familiar ways until at last her feet struck the dull solidity of the rotting pier. And then it was but a few more panting steps — and good

[176]

mother East River took Liz to her bosom, soothed her
muddily but quickly, and settled in five minutes the
problem that keeps lights burning o' nights in thousands of pastorates and colleges.

* * * * * *

It's mighty funny what kind of dreams one has
sometimes. Poets call them visions, but a vision is
only a dream in blank verse. I dreamed the rest of
this story.

I thought I was in the next world. I don't know
how I got there; I suppose I had been riding on the
Ninth avenue elevated or taking patent medicine or
trying to pull Jim Jeffries's nose, or doing some such
little injudicious stunt. But, anyhow, there I was,
and there was a great crowd of us outside the court-
room where the judgments were going on. And
every now and then a very beautiful and imposing
court-officer angel would come outside the door and
call another case.

While I was considering my own wordly sins and
wondering whether there would be any use of my trying to prove an alibi by claiming that I lived in New
Jersey, the bailiff angel came to the door and sang
out:

" Case No. 99,852,743."

Up stepped a plain-clothes man — there were lots
of 'em there, dressed exactly like preachers and hustling us spirits around just like cops do on earth —

and by the arm he dragged — whom, do you think?
Why, Liz!

The court officer took her inside and closed the
door. I went up to Mr. Fly-Cop and inquired about
the case.

"A very sad one," says he, laying the points of
his manicured fingers together. "An utterly incor-
rigible girl. I am Special Terrestrial Officer the Reverend Jones. The case was assigned to me. The
girl murdered her fiance and committed suicide. She
had no defense. My report to the court relates the
facts in detail, all of which are substantiated by re-
liable witnesses. The wages of sin is death. Praise
the Lord."

The court officer opened the door and stepped out.

"Poor girl," said Special Terrestrial Officer the
Reverend Jones, with a tear in his eye. "It was one
of the saddest cases that I ever met with. Of course
she was "———

"Discharged," said the court officer. "Come here,
Jonesy. First thing you know you'll be switched to
the pot-pie squad. How would you like to be on the
missionary force in the South Sea Islands — hey?
Now, you quit making these false arrests, or you'll be
transferred — see? The guilty party you've got to
look for in this case is a red-haired, unshaven, untidy
man, sitting by the window reading, in his stocking
feet, while his children play in the streets. Get a
move on you."

Now, wasn't that a silly dream?

ACCORDING TO THEIR LIGHTS

SOMEWHERE in the depths of the big city, where the unquiet dregs are forever being shaken together, young Murray and the Captain had met and become friends. Both were at the lowest ebb possible to their fortunes; both had fallen from at least an intermediate Heaven of respectability and importance, and both were typical products of the monstrous and peculiar social curriculum of their overweening and bumptious civic alma mater.

The captain was no longer a captain. One of those sudden moral cataclysms that sometimes sweep the city had hurled him from a high and profitable position in the Police Department, ripping off his badge and buttons and washing into the hands of his lawyers the solid pieces of real estate that his frugality had enabled him to accumulate. The passing of the flood left him low and dry. One month after his dishabilitation a saloon-keeper plucked him by the neck from his free-lunch counter as a tabby plucks a strange kitten from her nest, and cast him asphaltward. This seems low enough. But after that he acquired a pair of cloth top, button Congress gaiters and wrote complaining letters to the newspapers. And then he fought the attendant at the Municipal Lodging House who tried to give him a bath. When Murray first saw him he was holding the hand of an Italian woman who sold apples and garlic on Essex street, and quoting the words of a song book ballad.

Murray's fall had been more Luciferian, if less spectacular. All the pretty, tiny little kickshaws of Gotham had once been his. The megaphone man roars out at you to observe the house of his uncle on a grand and revered avenue. But there had been an awful row about something, and the prince had been escorted to the door by the butler, which, in said avenue, is equivalent to the impact of the avuncular shoe. A weak Prince Hal, without inheritance or sword, he drifted downward to meet his humorless Falstaff, and to pick the crusts of the streets with him.

One evening they sat on a bench in a little downtown park. The great bulk of the Captain, which starvation seemed to increase — drawing irony instead of pity to his petitions for aid — was heaped against the arm of the bench in a shapeless mass. His red face, spotted by tufts of vermillion, week-old whiskers and topped by a sagging white straw hat, looked, in the gloom, like one of those structures that you may observe in a dark Third avenue window, challenging your imagination to say whether it be something recent in the way of ladies' hats or a strawberry shortcake. A tight-drawn belt — last relic of his official spruceness — made a deep furrow in his circumference. The Captain's shoes were buttonless. In a smothered bass he cursed his star of ill-luck.

Murray, at his side, was shrunk into his dingy and ragged suit of blue serge. His hat was pulled low; he sat quiet and a little indistinct, like some ghost that had been dispossessed.

" I'm hungry," growled the Captain —" by the top sirloin of the Bull of Bashan, I'm starving to death. Right now I could eat a Bowery restaurant clear through to the stovepipe in the alley. Can't you think of nothing, Murray? You sit there with your shoulders scrunched up, giving an imitation of Reginald Vanderbilt driving his coach — what good are them airs doing you now? Think of some place we can get something to chew."

" You forget, my dear Captain," said Murray, without moving, " that our last attempt at dining was at my suggestion."

" You bet it was," groaned the Captain, " you bet your life it was. Have you got any more like that to make — hey? "

" I admit we failed," sighed Murray. " I was sure Malone would be good for one more free lunch after the way he talked baseball with me the last time I spent a nickel in his establishment."

"I had this hand," said the Captain, extending the unfortunate member —" I had this hand on the drumstick of a turkey and two sardine sandwiches when them waiters grabbed us."

"I was within two inches of the olives," said Murray. "Stuffed olives. I haven't tasted one in a year."

"What'll we do?" grumbled the Captain. "We can't starve."

"Can't we?" said Murray quietly. "I'm glad to hear that. I was afraid we could."

"You wait here," said the Captain, rising heavily and puffily to his feet. "I'm going to try to make one more turn. You stay here till I come back, Murray. I won't be over half an hour. If I turn the trick I'll come back flush."

He made some elephantine attempts at smartening his appearance. He gave his fiery mustache a heaven-ward twist; he dragged into sight a pair of black-edged cuffs, deepened the crease in his middle by tight-ening his belt another hole, and set off, jaunty as a zoo rhinoceros, across the south end of the park.

When he was out of sight Murray also left the park, hurrying swiftly eastward. He stopped at a building whose steps were flanked by two green lights.

"A police captain named Maroney," he said to the desk sergeant, "was dismissed from the force after being tried under charges three years ago. I believe sentence was suspended. Is this man wanted now by the police?"

"Why are ye asking?" inquired the sergeant, with a frown.

"I thought there might be a reward standing," explained Murray, easily. "I know the man well. He seems to be keeping himself pretty shady at present. I could lay my hands on him at any time. If there should be a reward——"

"There's no reward," interrupted the sergeant, shortly. "The man's not wanted. And neither are ye. So, get out. Ye are frindly with um, and ye would be selling um. Out with ye quick, or I'll give ye a start."

Murray gazed at the officer with serene and virtuous dignity.

"I would be simply doing my duty, as a citizen and gentleman," he said, severely, "if I should assist the law in laying hold of one of its offenders."

Murray hurried back to the bench in the park. He folded his arms and shrank within his clothes to his ghost-like presentment.

Ten minutes afterward the Captain arrived at the rendezvous, windy and thunderous as a dog-day in Kansas. His collar had been torn away; his straw hat had been twisted and battered; his shirt with ox-blood stripes split to the waist. And from head to knee he was drenched with some vile and ignoble greasy fluid that loudly proclaimed to the nose its component leaven of garlic and kitchen stuff.

" For Heaven's sake, Captain," sniffed Murray, " I doubt that I would have waited for you if I had suspected you were so desperate as to resort to swill barrels. I "——

" Cheese it," said the Captain, harshly. " I'm not hogging it yet. It's all on the outside. I went around on Essex and proposed marriage to that Catrina that's got the fruit shop there. Now, that business could be built up. She's a peach as far as a Dago could be. I thought I had that senoreena mashed sure last week. But look what she done to me! I guess I got too fresh. Well there's another scheme queered."

" You don't mean to say," said Murray, with infinite contempt, " that you would have married that woman to help yourself out of your disgraceful troubles! "

" Me? " said the Captain. " I'd marry the Empress of China for one bowl of chop suey. I'd commit murder for a plate of beef stew. I'd steal a wafer from a waif. I'd be a Mormon for a bowl of chowder."

" I think," said Murray, resting his head on his hands, " that I would play Judas for the price of one drink of whiskey. For thirty pieces of silver I would "——

" Oh, come now! " exclaimed the Captain in dismay. " You wouldn't do that, Murray? I always

[184]

thought that Kike's squeal on his boss was about the lowest-down play that ever happened. A man that gives his friend away is worse than a pirate."

Through the park stepped a large man scanning the benches where the electric light fell.

"Is that you, Mac?" he said, halting before the derelicts. His diamond stickpin dazzled. His diamond-studded fob chain assisted. He was big and smooth and well fed. "Yes, I see it's you," he continued. "They told me at Mike's that I might find you over here. Let me see you a few minutes, Mac."

The Captain lifted himself with a grunt of alacrity. If Charlie Finnegan had come down in the bottomless pit to seek him there must be something doing. Charlie guided him by an arm into a patch of shadow.

"You know, Mac," he said, "they're trying Inspector Pickering on graft charges."

"He was my inspector," said the Captain.

"O'Shea wants the job," went on Finnegan. "He must have it. It's for the good of the organization. Pickering must go under. Your testimony will do it. He was your 'man higher up' when you were on the force. His share of the boodle passed through your hands. You must go on the stand and testify against him."

"He was"— began the Captain.

"Wait a minute," said Finnegan. A bundle of
[185]

yellowish stuff came out of his inside pocket. " Five hundred dollars in it for you. Two-fifty on the spot, and the rest "——

" He was my friend, I say," finished the Captain. " I'll see you and the gang, and the city, and the party in the flames of Hades before I'll take the stand against Dan Pickering. I'm down and out; but I'm no traitor to a man that's been my friend." The Captain's voice rose and boomed like a split trombone. " Get out of this park, Charlie Finnegan, where us thieves and tramps and boozers are your betters; and take your dirty money with you."

Finnegan drifted out by another walk. The Captain returned to his seat.

" I couldn't avoid hearing," said Murray, drearily. " I think you are the biggest fool I ever saw."

" What would you have done? " asked the Captain.

" Nailed Pickering to the cross," said Murray.

" Sonny," said the Captain, huskily and without heat. " You and me are different. New York is divided into two parts — above Forty-second street, and below Fourteenth. You come from the other part. We both act according to our lights."

An illumiated clock above the trees retailed the information that it lacked the half hour of twelve. Both men rose from the bench and moved away together as if seized by the same idea. They left the park, struck through a narrow cross street, and came into Broadway, at this hour as dark, echoing and de-peopled as a byway in Pompeii.

Northward they turned; and a policeman who glanced at their unkempt and slinking figures with-held the attention and suspicion that he would have granted them at any other hour and place. For on every street in that part of the city other unkempt and slinking figures were shuffling and hurrying to-ward a converging point — a point that is marked by no monument save that groove on the pavement worn by tens of thousands of waiting feet.

At Ninth street a tall man wearing an opera hat alighted from a Broadway car and turned his face westward. But he saw Murray, pounced upon him and dragged him under a street light. The Captain lumbered slowly to the corner, like a wounded bear, and waited, growling.

" Jerry ! " cried the hatted one. " How fortunate ! I was to begin a search for you to-morrow. The old gentleman has capitulated. You're to be restored to favor. Congratulate you. Come to the office in the morning and get all the money you want. I've liberal instructions in that respect."

" And the little matrimonial arrangement? " said Murray, with his head turned sidewise.

" Why — er — well, of course, your uncle understands — expects that the engagement between you Miss Vanderhurst shall be "——

" Good-night! " said Murray, moving away.

" You madman! " cried the other, catching his arm. " Would you give up two millions on account of "——

" Did you ever see her nose, old man? " asked Murray, solemnly.

" But, listen to reason, Jerry. Miss Vanderhurst is an heiress, and "——

" Did you ever see it? "

" Yes, I admit that her nose isn't "——

" Good night! " said Murray. " My friend is waiting for me. I am quoting him when I authorize you to report that there is ' nothing doing.' Good night."

A wriggling line of waiting men extended from a door in Tenth street far up Broadway, on the outer edge of the pavement. The Captain and Murray fell in at the tail of the quivering millipede.

" Twenty feet longer than it was last night," said Murray, looking up at his measuring angle of Grace Church.

" Half an hour," growled the Captain, " before we get our punk."

The city clocks began to strike 12; the Bread Line moved forward slowly, its leathern feet sliding on the stones with the sound of a hissing serpent, as they who had lived according to their lights closed up in the rear.

A MIDSUMMER KNIGHT'S DREAM

> " *The knights are dead;*
> *Their swords are rust.*
> *Except a few who have to hust-*
> *Le all the time*
> *To raise the dust.*"

DEAR READER: It was summertime. The sun glared down upon the city with pitiless ferocity. It is difficult for the sun to be ferocious and exhibit compunction simultaneously. The heat was — oh, bother thermometers! — who cares for standard measures, anyhow? It was so hot that —

The roof gardens put on so many extra waiters that you could hope to get your gin fizz now — as soon as all the other people got theirs. The hospitals were putting in extra cots for bystanders. For when little woolly dogs loll their tongues out and say " woof, woof! " at the fleas that bite 'em, and nervous old black bombazine ladies screech " Mad dog! " and policemen begin to shoot, somebody is going to get hurt. The man from Pompton, N. J., who always wears an overcoat in July, had turned up in a Broadway hotel drinking hot Scotches and enjoying his annual ray from the calcium. Philanthropists

[189]

were petitioning the Legislature to pass a bill requiring builders to make tenement fire-escapes more com-
modious, so that families might die all together of
the heat instead of one or two at a time. So many
men were telling you about the number of baths they
took each day that you wondered how they got along
after the real lessee of the apartment came back to
town and thanked 'em for taking such good care of
it. The young man who called loudly for cold beef
and beer in the restaurant, protesting that roast pul-
let and Burgundy was really too heavy for such
weather, blushed when he met your eye, for you had
heard him all winter calling, in modest tones, for the
same ascetic viands. Soup, pocketbooks, shirt waists,
actors and baseball excuses grew thinner. Yes, it was
summertime.

A man stood at Thirty-fourth street waiting for
for a downtown car. A man of forty, gray-haired,
pink-faced, keen, nervous, plainly dressed, with a har-
assed look around the eyes. He wiped his forehead
and laughed loudly when a fat man with an outing
look stopped and spoke with him.

"No, siree," he shouted with defiance and scorn.
"None of your old mosquito-haunted swamps and
skyscraper mountains without elevators for me.
When I want to get away from hot weather I know
how to do it. New York, sir, is the finest summer resort in the country. Keep in the shade and watch

your diet, and don't get too far away from an electric fan. Talk about your Adirondacks and your Catskills! There's more solid comfort in the borough of Manhattan than in all the rest of the country together. No, siree! No tramping up perpendicular cliffs and being waked up at 4 in the morning by a million flies, and eating canned goods straight from the city for me. Little old New York will take a few select summer boarders; comforts and conveniences of homes — that's the ad. that I answer every time."

" You need a vacation," said the fat man, looking closely at the other. " You haven't been away from town in years. Better come with me for two weeks, anyhow. The trout in the Beaverkill are jumping at anything now that looks like a fly. Harding writes me that he landed a three-pound brown last week."

" Nonsense! " cried the other man. " Go ahead, if you like, and boggle around in rubber boots wearing yourself out trying to catch fish. When I want one I go to a cool restaurant and order it. I laugh at you fellows whenever I think of you hustling around in the heat in the country thinking you are having a good time. For me Father Knickerbocker's little improved farm with the big shady lane running through the middle of it."

The fat man sighed over his friend and went his way. The man who thought New York was the greatest summer resort in the country boarded a car and went buzzing down to his office. On the way he threw away his newspaper and looked up at a ragged patch of sky above the housetops.

" Three pounds!" he muttered, absently. " And Harding isn't a liar. I believe, if I could — but it's impossible — they've got to have another month — another month at least."

In his office the upholder of urban midsummer joys dived, headforemost, into the swimming pool of business. Adkins, his clerk, came and added a spray of letters, memoranda and telegrams.

At 5 o'clock in the afternoon the busy man leaned back in his office chair, put his feet on the desk and mused aloud:

" I wonder what kind of bait Harding used."

* * * * * * * *

She was all in white that day; and thereby Compton lost a bet to Gaines. Compton had wagered she would wear light blue, for she knew that was his favorite color, and Compton was a millionaire's son, and that almost laid him open to the charge of betting on a sure thing. But white was her choice, and Gaines held up his head with twenty-five's lordly air.

The little summer hotel in the mountains had a lively crowd that year. There were two or three young college men and a couple of artists and a young naval officer on one side. On the other there were enough beauties among the young ladies for the correspondent of a society paper to refer to them as a " bevy." But the moon among the stars was Mary Sewell. Each one of the young men greatly desired to arrange matters so that he could pay her millinery bills, and fix the furnace, and have her do away with the " Sewell " part of her name forever. Those who could stay only a week or two went away hinting at pistols and blighted hearts. But Compton stayed like the mountains themselves, for he could afford it. And Gaines stayed because he was a fighter and wasn't afraid of millionaire's sons, and — well, he adored the country.

" What do you think, Miss Mary? " he said once. " I knew a duffer in New York who claimed to like it in the summer time. Said you could keep cooler there than you could in the woods. Wasn't he an awful silly? I don't think I could breathe on Broadway after the 1st of June."

" Mamma was thinking of going back week after next," said Miss Mary with a lovely frown.

" But when you think of it," said Gaines, " there are lots of jolly places in town in the summer. The roof gardens, you know, and the — er — the roof gardens."

Deepest blue was the lake that day — the day when they had the mock tournament, and the men rode clumsy farm horses around in a glade in the woods and caught curtain rings on the end of a lance.   Such fun!

Cool and dry as the finest wine came the breath of the shadowed forest.   The valley below was a vision seen through an opal haze.   A white mist from hidden falls blurred the green of a hand's breath of tree tops half-way down the gorge.   Youth made merry hand-in-hand with young summer.   Nothing on Broadway like that.

The villagers gathered to see the city folks pursue their mad drollery.   The woods rang with the laughter of pixies and naiads and sprites.   Gaines caught most of the rings.   His was the privilege to crown the queen of the tournament.   He was the conquering knight — as far as the rings went.   On his arm he wore a white scarf.   Compton wore light blue.   She had declared her preference for blue, but she wore white that day.

Gaines looked about for the queen to crown her. He heard her merry laugh, as if from the clouds. She had slipped away and climbed Chimney Rock, a little granite bluff, and stood there, a white fairy among the laurels, fifty feet above their heads.

Instantly he and Compton accepted the implied challenge.   The bluff was easily mounted at the rear, but the front offered small hold to hand or foot. Each man quickly selected his route and began to climb.   A crevice, a bush, a slight projection, a vine or tree branch — all of these were aids that counted in the race. It was all foolery — there was no stake; but there was youth in it, cross reader, and light hearts, and something else that Miss Clay writes so charmingly about.

Gaines gave a great tug at the root of a laurel and pulled himself to Miss Mary's feet. On his arm he carried the wreath of roses; and while the villagers and summer boarders screamed and applauded below he placed it on the queen's brow.

" You are a gallant knight," said Miss Mary.

" If I could be your true knight always," began Gaines, but Miss Mary laughed him dumb, for Compton scrambled over the edge of the rock one minute behind time.

What a twilight that was when they drove back to the hotel! The opal of the valley turned slowly to purple, the dark woods framed the lake as a mirror, the tonic air stirred the very soul in one. The first pale stars came out over the mountain tops where yet a faint glow of ——

   *   *   *   *   *   *   *   *

" I beg your pardon, Mr. Gaines," said Adkins.

The man who believed New York to be the finest summer resort in the world opened his eyes and kicked over the mucilage bottle on his desk.

" I — I believe I was asleep," he said.

" It's the heat," said Adkins. " It's something awful in the city these "——

" Nonsense! " said the other. " The city beats the country ten to one in summer. Fools go out tramping in muddy brooks and wear themselves out trying to catch little fish as long as your finger. Stay in town and keep comfortable — that's my idea."

" Some letters just came," said Adkins. " I thought you might like to glance at them before you go."

Let us look over his shoulder and read just a few lines of one of them:

MY DEAR, DEAR HUSBAND: Just received your letter ordering us to stay another month. . . . . . . Rita's cough is almost gone. . . . Johnny has simply gone wild like a little Indian. . . . Will be the making of both children. . . . work so hard, and I know that your business can hardly afford to keep us here so long. . . . best man that ever . . . you always pretend that you like the city in summer. . . . trout fishing that you used to be so fond of . . . and all to keep us well and happy . . . come to you if it were not doing the babies so much good. . . . I stood last evening on Chimney Rock in exactly the same spot where I was when you put the wreath of roses on my head. . . . through all the world . . .

when you said you would be my true knight . . .
fifteen years ago, dear, just think! . . . have
always been that to me . . . ever and ever,

MARY.

The man who said he thought New York the finest
summer resort in the country dropped into a café on
his way home and had a glass of beer under an electric fan.

"Wonder what kind of a fly old Harding used,"
he said to himself.

THE LAST LEAF

IN a little district west of Washington Square the streets have run crazy and broken themselves into small strips called " places." These " places " make strange angles and curves. One street crosses itself a time or two. An artist once discovered a valuable possibility in this street. Suppose a collector with a bill for paints, paper and canvas should, in traversing this route, suddenly meet himself coming back, without a cent having been paid on account!

So, to quaint old Greenwich Village the art people soon came prowling, hunting for north windows and eighteenth-century gables and Dutch attics and low rents. Then they imported some pewter mugs and a chafing dish or two from Sixth avenue, and became a " colony."

At the top of a squatty, three-story brick Sue and Johnsy had their studio. " Johnsy " was familiar for Joanna. One was from Maine; the other from California. They had met at the *table d'hote* of an Eighth street " Delmonico's," and found their tastes in art, chicory salad and bishop sleeves so congenial that the joint studio resulted.

That was in May. In November a cold, unseen

stranger, whom the doctors called Pneumonia, stalked about the colony, touching one here and there with his icy finger. Over on the east side this ravager strode boldly, smiting his victims by scores, but his feet trod slowly through the maze of the narrow and moss-grown " places."

Mr. Pneumonia was not what you would call a chivalric old gentleman. A mite of a little woman with blood thinned by California zephyrs was hardly fair game for the red-fisted, short-breathed old duffer. But Johnsy he smote; and she lay, scarcely moving, on her painted iron bedstead, looking through the small Dutch window-panes at the blank side of the next brick house.

One morning the busy doctor invited Sue into the hallway with a shaggy, gray eyebrow.

" She has one chance in — let us say, ten," he said; as he shook down the mercury in his clinical ther-mometer. " And that chance is for her to want to live. This way people have of lining-up on the side of the undertaker makes the entire pharmacopeia look silly. Your little lady has made up her mind that she's not going to get well. Has she anything on her mind? "

" She — she wanted to paint the Bay of Naples some day," said Sue.

" Paint? — bosh! Has she anything on her mind worth thinking about twice — a man, for instance? "

" A man? " said Sue, with a jewsharp twang in her voice. " Is a man worth — but, no, doctor; there is nothing of the kind."

" Well, it is the weakness, then," said the doctor. " I will do all that science, so far as it may filter through my efforts, can accomplish. But whenever my patient begins to count the carriages in her funeral procession I subtract 50 per cent. from the curative power of medicines. If you will get her to ask one question about the new winter styles in cloak sleeves I will promise you a one-in-five chance for her, instead of one in ten."

After the doctor had gone Sue went into the workroom and cried a Japanese napkin to a pulp. Then she swaggered into Johnsy's room with her drawing board, whistling ragtime.

Johnsy lay, scarcely making a ripple under the bedclothes, with her face toward the window. Sue stopped whistling, thinking she was asleep.

She arranged her board and began a pen-and-ink drawing to illustrate a magazine story. Young artists must pave their way to Art by drawing pictures for magazine stories that young authors write to pave their way to Literature.

As Sue was sketching a pair of elegant horse-show riding trousers and a monocle on the figure of the hero, an Idaho cowboy, she heard a low sound, several times repeated. She went quickly to the bed-side.

Johnsy's eyes were open wide. She was looking out the window and counting — counting backward.

"Twelve," she said, and a little later "eleven;" and then "ten," and "nine;" and then "eight" and "seven," almost together.

Sue looked solicitously out the window. What was there to count? There was only a bare, dreary yard to be seen, and the blank side of the brick house twenty feet away. An old, old ivy vine, gnarled and decayed at the roots, climbed half way up the brick wall. The cold breath of autumn had stricken its leaves from the vine until its skeleton branches clung, almost bare, to the crumbling bricks.

"What is it, dear?" asked Sue.

"Six," said Johnsy, in almost a whisper. "They're falling faster now. Three days ago there were almost a hundred. It made my head ache to count them. But now it's easy. There goes another one. There are only five left now."

"Five what, dear. Tell your Sudie.'

"Leaves. On the ivy vine. When the last one falls I must go, too. I've known that for three days. Didn't the doctor tell you?"

"Oh, I never heard of such nonsense," complained Sue, with magnificent scorn. "What have old ivy leaves to do with your getting well? And you used

[201]

to love that vine so, you naughty girl. Don't be a
goosey. Why, the doctor told me this morning that
your chances for getting well real soon were — let's
see exactly what he said — he said the chances were
ten to one! Why, that's almost as good a chance as
we have in New York when we ride on the street
cars or walk past a new building. Try to take some
broth now, and let Sudie go back to her drawing, so
she can sell the editor man with it, and buy port wine
for her sick child, and pork chops for her greedy
self."

"You needn't get any more wine," said Johnsy,
keeping her eyes fixed out the window. "There goes
another. No, I don't want any broth. That leaves
just four. I want to see the last one fall before it
gets dark. Then I'll go, too."

"Johnsy, dear," said Sue, bending over her, "will
you promise me to keep your eyes closed, and not
look out the window until I am done working? I
must hand those drawings in by to-morrow. I need
the light, or I would draw the shade down."

"Couldn't you draw in the other room?" asked
Johnsy, coldly.

"I'd rather be here by you," said Sue. "Besides,
I don't want you to keep looking at those silly ivy
leaves."

"Tell me as soon as you have finished," said
Johnsy, closing her eyes, and lying white and still as

a fallen statue, " because I want to see the last one fall. I'm tired of waiting. I'm tired of thinking. I want to turn loose my hold on everything, and go sailing down, down, just like one of those poor, tired leaves."

" Try to sleep," said Sue. " I must call Behrman up to be my model for the old hermit miner. I'll not be gone a minute. Don't try to move 'till I come back."

Old Behrman was a painter who lived on the ground floor beneath them. He was past sixty and had a Michael Angelo's Moses beard curling down from the head of a satyr along the body of an imp. Behrman was a failure in art. Forty years he had wielded the brush without getting near enough to touch the hem of his Mistress's robe. He had been always about to paint a masterpiece, but had never yet begun it. For several years he had painted nothing except now and then a daub in the line of commerce or advertising. He earned a little by serving as a model to those young artists in the colony who could not pay the price of a professional. He drank gin to excess, and still talked of his coming masterpiece. For the rest he was a fierce little old man, who scoffed terribly at softness in any one, and who regarded himself as especial mastiff-in-waiting to protect the two young artists in the studio above.

Sue found Behrman smelling strongly of juniper

berries in his dimly lighted den below. In one corner was a blank canvas on an easel that had been waiting there for twenty-five years to receive the first line of the masterpiece. She told him of Johnsy's fancy, and how she feared she would, indeed, light and fragile as a leaf herself, float away when her slight hold upon the world grew weaker.

Old Behrman, with his red eyes plainly streaming, shouted his contempt and derision for such idiotic imaginings.

"Vass!" he cried. "Is dere people in de world mit der foolishness to die because leafs dey drop off from a confounded vine? I haf not heard of such a thing. No, I vill not bose as a model for your fool hermit-dunderhead. Vy do you allow dot silly pusiness to come in der prain of her? Ach, dot poor lettle Miss Johnsy."

"She is very ill and weak," said Sue, "and the fever has left her mind morbid and full of strange fancies. Very well, Mr. Behrman, if you do not care to pose for me, you needn't. But I think you are a horrid old — old flibbertigibbet."

"You are just like a woman!" yelled Behrman. "Who said I vill not bose? Go on. I come mit you. For half an hour I haf peen trying to say dot I am ready to bose. Gott! dis is not any blace in which one so goot as Miss Yohnsy shall lie sick.

Some day I vill baint a masterpiece, and ve shall all
go avay. Gott! yes."

Johnsy was sleeping when they went upstairs. Sue
pulled the shade down to the window-sill, and mo-
tioned Behrman into the other room. In **there** they
peered out the window fearfully at the ivy vine.
Then they looked at each other for a moment without speaking. A persistent, cold rain was falling,
mingled with snow. Behrman, in his old blue shirt,
took his seat as the hermit-miner on an upturned
kettle for a rock.

When Sue awoke from an hour's sleep the next
morning she found Johnsy with dull, wide-open eyes
staring at the drawn green shade.

" Pull it up; I want to see," she ordered, in a
whisper.

Wearily Sue obeyed.

But, lo! after the beating rain and fierce gusts of
wind that had endured through the livelong night,
there yet stood out against the brick wall one ivy
leaf. It was the last on the vine. Still dark green
near its stem, but with its serrated edges tinted with
the yellow of dissolution and decay, it hung bravely
from a branch some twenty feet above the ground.

"It is the last one," said Johnsy. "I thought it
would surely fall during the night. I heard the wind.
It will fall to-day, and I shall die at the same time."

"Dear, dear!" said Sue, leaning her worn face

down to the pillow, " think of me, if you won't think
of yourself. What would I do? "

But Johnsy did not answer. The lonesomest thing
in all the world is a soul when it is making ready
to go on its mysterious, far journey. The fancy
seemed to possess her more strongly as one by one
the ties that bound her to friendship and to earth
were loosed.

The day wore away, and even through the twilight
they could see the lone ivy leaf clinging to its stem
against the wall. And then, with the coming of the
night the north wind was again loosed, while the rain
still beat against the windows and pattered down from
the low Dutch eaves.

When it was light enough Johnsy, the merciless,
commanded that the shade be raised.

The ivy leaf was still there.

Johnsy lay for a long time looking at it. And then
she called to Sue, who was stirring her chicken broth
over the gas stove.

" I've been a bad girl, Sudie," said Johnsy.
" Something has made that last leaf stay there to show
me how wicked I was. It is a sin to want to die.
You may bring me a little broth now, and some milk
with a little port in it, and — no; bring me a hand-
mirror first; and then pack some pillows about me,
and I will sit up and watch you cook."

An hour later she said.

"Sudie, some day I hope to paint the Bay of Naples."

The doctor came in the afternoon, and Sue had an excuse to go into the hallway as he left.

"Even chances," said the doctor, taking Sue's thin, shaking hand in his. "With good nursing you'll win. And now I must see another case I have downstairs. Behrman, his name is — some kind of an artist, I believe. Pneumonia, too. He is an old, weak man, and the attack is acute. There is no hope for him; but he goes to the hospital to-day to be made more comfortable."

The next day the doctor said to Sue: "She's out of danger. You've won. Nutrition and care now — that's all."

And that afternoon Sue came to the bed where Johnsy lay, contentedly knitting a very blue and very useless woolen shoulder scarf, and put one arm around her, pillows and all.

"I have something to tell you, white mouse," she said. "Mr. Behrman died of pneumonia to-day in the hospital. He was ill only two days. The janitor found him on the morning of the first day in his room downstairs helpless with pain. His shoes and clothing were wet through and icy cold. They couldn't imagine where he had been on such a dreadful night. And then they found a lantern, still lighted, and a ladder that had been dragged from its place, and some scattered brushes, and a palette with green and yellow colors mixed on it, and — look out the window, dear, at the last ivy leaf on the wall. Didn't you wonder why it never fluttered or moved when the wind blew? Ah, darling, it's Behrman's masterpiece — he painted it there the night that the last leaf fell."

THE COUNT AND THE WEDDING GUEST

ONE evening when Andy Donovan went to dinner at his Second Avenue boarding-house, Mrs. Scott introduced him to a new boarder, a young lady, Miss Conway. Miss Conway was small and unobtrusive. She wore a plain, snuffy-brown dress, and bestowed her interest, which seemed languid, upon her plate. She lifted her diffident eyelids and shot one perspicuous, judicial glance at Mr. Donovan, politely murmured his name, and returned to her mutton. Mr. Donovan bowed with the grace and beaming smile that were rapidly winning for him social, business and political advancement, and erased the snuffy-brown one from the tablets of his consideration.

Two weeks later Andy was sitting on the front steps enjoying his cigar. There was a soft rustle behind and above him, and Andy turned his head — and had his head turned.

Just coming out the door was Miss Conway. She wore a night-black dress of *crepe de — crepe de —* oh, this thin black goods. Her hat was black, and from it drooped and fluttered an ebon veil, filmy as a spider's web. She stood on the top step and drew on black silk gloves. Not a speck of white or a spot

of color about her dress anywhere. Her rich golden
hair was drawn, with scarcely a ripple, into a shining,
smooth knot low on her neck. Her face was plain
rather than pretty, but it was now illuminated and
made almost beautiful by her large gray eyes that
gazed above the houses across the street into the sky
with an expression of the most appealing sadness and
melancholy.

Gather the idea, girls — all black, you know, with
the preference for *crêpe de* — oh, *crêpe de Chine* —
that's it. All black, and that sad, faraway look, and
the hair shining under the black veil (you have to be
a blonde, of course), and try to look as if, although
your young life had been blighted just as it was about
to give a hop-skip-and-a-jump over the threshold of
life, a walk in the park might do you good, and be
sure to happen out the door at the right moment, and
— oh, it'll fetch 'em every time. But it's fierce, now,
how cynical I am, ain't it? — to talk about mourning
costumes this way.

Mr. Donovan suddenly reinscribed Miss Conway
upon the tablets of his consideration. He threw away
the remaining inch-and-a-quarter of his cigar, that
would have been good for eight minutes yet, and
quickly shifted his center of gravity to his low cut
patent leathers.

"It's a fine, clear evening, Miss Conway," he said;
and if the Weather Bureau could have heard the con-

fident emphasis of his tones it would have hoisted the square white signal, and nailed it to the mast.

"To them that has the heart to enjoy it, it is, Mr. Donovan," said Miss Conway, with a sigh.

Mr. Donovan, in his heart, cursed fair weather. Heartless weather! It should hail and blow and snow to be consonant with the mood of Miss Conway.

"I hope none of your relatives — I hope you haven't sustained a loss?" ventured Mr. Donovan.

"Death has claimed," said Miss Conway, hesitating — "not a relative, but one who — but I will not intrude my grief upon you, Mr. Donovan."

"Intrude?" protested Mr. Donovan. "Why, say, Miss Conway, I'd be delighted, that is, I'd be sorry — I mean I'm sure nobody could sympathize with you truer than I would."

Miss Conway smiled a little smile. And oh, it was sadder than her expression in repose.

"'Laugh, and the world laughs with you; weep, and they give you the laugh,'" she quoted. "I have learned that, Mr. Donovan. I have no friends or acquaintances in this city. But you have been kind to me. I appreciate it highly."

He had passed her the pepper twice at the table.

"It's tough to be alone in New York — that's a cinch," said Mr. Donovan. "But, say — whenever this little old town does loosen up and get friendly it goes the limit. Say you took a little stroll in the park, Miss Conway — don't you think it might chase away some of your mullygrubs? And if you'd allow me —"

" Thanks, Mr. Donovan. I'd be pleased to accept of your escort if you think the company of one whose heart is filled with gloom could be anyways agreeable to you."

Through the open gates of the iron-railed, old, downtown park, where the elect once took the air, they strolled, and found a quiet bench.

There is this difference between the grief of youth and that of old age; youth's burden is lightened by as much of it as another shares; old age may give and give, but the sorrow remains the same.

" He was my fiance," confided Miss Conway, at the end of an hour. " We were going to be married next spring. I don't want you to think that I am stringing you, Mr. Donovan, but he was a real Count. He had an estate and a castle in Italy. Count Fernando Mazzini was his name. I never saw the beat of him for elegance. Papa objected, of course, and once we eloped, but papa overtook us, and took us back. I thought sure papa and Fernando would fight a duel. Papa has a livery business — in P'kipsee, you know.

" Finally, papa came 'round, all right, and said we might be married next spring. Fernando showed him proofs of his title and wealth, and then went over to Italy to get the castle fixed up for us. Papa's very proud, and when Fernando wanted to give me several thousand dollars for my trousseau he called him down something awful. He wouldn't even let me take a ring or any presents from him. And when Fernando sailed I came to the city and got a position as cashier in a candy store.

" Three days ago I got a letter from Italy, forwarded from P'kipsee, saying that Fernando had been killed in a gondola accident.

" That is why I am in mourning. My heart, Mr. Donovan, will remain forever in his grave. I guess I am poor company, Mr. Donovan, but I cannot take any interest in no one. I should not care to keep you from gayety and your friends who can smile and entertain you. Perhaps you would prefer to walk back to the house? "

Now, girls, if you want to observe a young man hustle out after a pick and shovel, just tell him that your heart is in some other fellow's grave. Young men are grave-robbers by nature. Ask any widow. Something must be done to restore that missing organ to weeping angels in *crêpe de Chine*. Dead men certainly got the worst of it from all sides.

" I'm awful sorry," said Mr. Donovan, gently. " No, we won't walk back to the house just yet. And don't say you haven't no friends in this city, Miss Conway. I'm awful sorry, and I want you to believe I'm your friend, and that I'm awful sorry."

[213]

"I've got his picture here in my locket," said Miss Conway, after wiping her eyes with her handkerchief. "I never showed it to anybody; but I will to you, Mr. Donovan, because I believe you to be a true friend."

Mr. Donovan gazed long and with much interest at the photograph in the locket that Miss Conway opened for him. The face of Count Mazzini was one to command interest. It was a smooth, intelligent, bright, almost a handsome face — the face of a strong, cheerful man who might well be a leader among his fellows.

"I have a larger one, framed, in my room," said Miss Conway. "When we return I will show you that. They are all I have to remind me of Fernando. But he ever will be present in my heart, that's a sure thing."

A subtle task confronted Mr. Donovan — that of supplanting the unfortunate Count in the heart of Miss Conway. This his admiration for her determined him to do. But the magnitude of the undertaking did not seem to weigh upon his spirits. The sympathetic but cheerful friend was the rôle he essayed; and he played it so successfully that the next half-hour found them conversing pensively across two plates of ice-cream, though yet there was no diminution of the sadness in Miss Conway's large gray eyes.

Before they parted in the hall that evening she ran

upstairs and brought down the framed photograph wrapped lovingly in a white silk scarf. Mr. Donovan surveyed it with inscrutable eyes.

" He gave me this the night he left for Italy," said Miss Conway. " I had the one for the locket made from this."

" A fine-looking man," said Mr. Donovan, heartily. " How would it suit you, Miss Conway, to give me pleasure of your company to Coney next Sunday afternoon? "

A month later they announced their engagement to Mrs. Scott and the other boarders. Miss Conway continued to wear black.

A week after the announcement the two sat on the same bench in the downtown park, while the fluttering leaves of the trees made a dim kinetoscopic picture of them in the moonlight. But Donovan had worn a look of abstracted gloom all day. He was so silent to-night that love's lips could not keep back any longer the questions that love's heart propounded.

" What's the matter, Andy, you are so solemn and grouchy to-night? "

" Nothing, Maggie."

" I know better. Can't I tell? You never acted this way before. What is it?

" It's nothing much, Maggie."

" Yes it is; and I want to know. I'll bet it's some other girl you are thinking about. All right. Why

don't you go get her if you want her? Take your
arm away, if you please."

"I'll tell you then," said Andy, wisely, "but I
guess you won't understand it exactly. You've heard
of Mike Sullivan, haven't you? 'Big Mike' Sullivan, everybody calls him."

"No, I haven't," said Maggie. "And I don't want
to, if he makes you act like this. Who is he?"

"He's the biggest man in New York," said Andy,
almost reverently. "He can about do anything he
wants to with Tammany or any other old thing in
the political line. He's a mile high and as broad as
East River. You say anything against Big Mike,
and you'll have a million men on your collarbone in
about two seconds. Why, he made a visit over to the
old country awhile back, and the kings took to their
holes like rabbits.

"Well, Big Mike's a friend of mine. I ain't more
than deuce-high in the district as far as influence
goes, but Mike's as good a friend to a little man, or
a poor man as he is to a big one. I met him to-day
on the Bowery, and what do you think he does?
Comes up and shakes hands. 'Andy,' says he, 'I've
been keeping cases on you. You've been putting in
some good licks over on your side of the street, and
I'm proud of you. What'll you take to drink?' He
takes a cigar, and I take a highball. I told him
I was going to get married in two weeks. 'Andy,'

says he, ' send me an invitation, so I'll keep in mind
of it, and I'll come to the wedding.' That's what
Big Mike says to me; and he always does what he
says.

" You don't understand it, Maggie, but I'd have
one of my hands cut off to have Big Mike Sullivan at
our wedding. It would be the proudest day of my
life. When he goes to a man's wedding, there's a guy
being married that's made for life. Now, that's why
I've maybe looking sore to-night."

" Why don't you invite him, then, if he's so much
to the mustard? " said Maggie, lightly.

" There's a reason why I can't," said Andy, sadly.
" There's a reason why he mustn't be there. Don't
ask me what it is, for I can't tell you."

" Oh, I don't care," said Maggie. " It's something
about politics, of course. But it's no reason why you
can't smile at me."

" Maggie," said Andy, presently, " do you think as
much of me as you did of your — as you did of the
Count Mazzini? "

He waited a long time, but Maggie did not reply.
And then, suddenly she leaned against his shoulder
and began to cry — to cry and shake with sobs, holding his arm tightly, and wetting the *crêpe de Chine*
with tears.

" There, there, there! " soothed Andy, putting aside
his own trouble. " And what is it, now? "

"Andy," sobbed Maggie. "I've lied to you, and you'll never marry me, or love me any more. But I feel that I've got to tell. Andy, there never was so much as the little finger of a count. I never had a beau in my life. But all the other girls had; and they talked about 'em; and that seemed to make the fellows like 'em more. And, Andy, I look swell in black — you know I do. So I went out to a photograph store and bought that picture, and had a little one made for my locket, and made up all that story about the Count, and about his being killed, so I could wear black. And nobody can love a liar, and you'll shake me, Andy, and I'll die for shame. Oh, there never was anybody I liked but you — and that's all."

But instead of being pushed away, she found Andy's arm folding her closer. She looked up and saw his face cleared and smiling.

"Could you — could you forgive me, Andy?"

"Sure," said Andy. "It's all right about that. Back to the cemetery for the Count. You've straightened everything out, Maggie. I was in hopes you would before the wedding-day. Bully girl!"

"Andy," said Maggie, with a somewhat shy smile, after she had been thoroughly assured of forgiveness, "did you believe all that story about the Count?"

"Well, not to any large extent," said Andy, reaching for his cigar case; "because it's Big Mike Sullivan's picture you've got in that locket of yours."

THE COUNTRY OF ELUSION

THE cunning writer will choose an indefinable subject, for he can then set down his theory of what it is;
and next, at length, his conception of what it is not
— and lo! his paper is covered. Therefore let us follow the prolix and unmapable trail into that mooted
country, Bohemia.

Grainger, sub-editor of *Doe's Magazine*, closed his
roll-top desk, put on his hat, walked into the hall,
punched the "down" button, and waited for the
elevator.

Grainger's day had been trying. The chief had
tried to ruin the magazine a dozen times by going
against Grainger's ideas for running it. A lady
whose grandfather had fought with McClellan had
brought a portfolio of poems in person.

Grainger was curator of the Lion's House of the
magazine. That day he had "lunched" an Arctic
explorer, a short-story writer, and the famous con-
ductor of a slaughter-house exposé. Consequently his
mind was in a whirl of icebergs, Maupassant, and
trichinosis.

But there was a surcease and a recourse; there was

THE TRIMMED LAMP

Bohemia. He would seek distraction there; and, let's see — he would call by for Mary Adrian.

Half an hour later he threaded his way like a Brazilian orchid-hunter through the palm forest in the tiled entrance hall of the " Idealia " apartment-house. One day the christeners of apartment-houses and the cognominators of sleeping-cars will meet, and there will be some jealous and sanguinary knifing.

The clerk breathed Grainger's name so languidly into the house telephone that it seemed it must surely drop, from sheer inertia, down to the janitor's regions. But, at length, it soared dilatorily up to Miss Adrian's ear. Certainly, Mr. Grainger was to come up immediately.

A colored maid with an Eliza-crossing-the-ice expression opened the door of the apartment for him. Grainger walked sideways down the narrow hall. A bunch of burnt umber hair and a sea-green eye appeared in the crack of a door. A long, white, undraped arm came out, barring the way.

" So glad you came, Ricky, instead of any of the others," said the eye. " Light a cigarette and give it to me. Going to take me to dinner? Fine. Go into the front room till I finish dressing. But don't sit in your usual chair. There's pie in it — Meringue. Kappelman threw it at Reeves last evening while he was reciting. Sophy has just come to straighten up. Is it lit? Thanks. There's Scotch

on the mantel — oh, no, it isn't — that's chartreuse.
Ask Sophy to find you some. I won't be long."

Grainger escaped the meringue. As he waited his
spirits sank still lower. The atmosphere of the room
was as vapid as a zephyr wandering over a Vesuvian
lava-bed. Relics of some feast lay about the room,
scattered in places where even a prowling cat would
have been surprised to find them. A straggling cluster of deep red roses in a marmalade jar bowed their
heads over tobacco ashes and unwashed goblets. A
chafing-dish stood on the piano; a leaf of sheet music
supported a stack of sandwiches in a chair.

Mary came in, dressed and radiant. Her gown
was of that thin, black fabric whose name through
the change of a single vowel seems to summon visions ranging between the extremes of man's experience.
Spelled with an " *ê* " it belongs to Gallic witchery and
diaphanous dreams; with an " a " it drapes lamenta-
tion and woe.

That evening they went to the Café André. And,
as people would confide to you in a whisper that
André's was the only truly Bohemian restaurant in
town, it may be well to follow them.

André began his professional career as a waiter in
a Bowery ten-cent eating-house. Had you seen him
there you would have called him tough — to yourself.
Not aloud, for he would have " soaked " you as
quickly as he would have soaked his thumb in your

coffee. He saved money and started a basement *table d'hôte* in Eighth (or Ninth) Street. One afternoon André drank too much absinthe. He announced to his startled family that he was the Grand Llama of Thibet, therefore requiring an empty audience hall in which to be worshiped. He moved all the tables and chairs from the restaurant into the back yard, wrapped a red table-cloth around himself, and sat on a step-ladder for a throne. When the diners began to arrive, madame, in a flurry of despair, laid cloths and ushered them, trembling, outside. Between the tables clothes-lines were stretched, bearing the family wash. A party of Bohemia hunters greeted the artistic innovation with shrieks and acclamations of delight. That week's washing was not taken in for two years. When André came to his senses he had the menu printed on stiffly starched cuffs, and served the ices in little wooden tubs. Next he took down his sign and darkened the front of the house. When you went there to dine you fumbled for an electric button and pressed it. A lookout slid open a panel in the door, looked at you suspiciously, and asked if you were acquainted with Senator Herodotus Q. McMilligan, of the Chickasaw Nation. If you were, you were admitted and allowed to dine. If you were not, you were admitted and allowed to dine. There you have one of the abiding principles of Bohemia. When André had accumulated $20,000 he moved uptown, near Broadway, in the fierce light that beats upon the thrown-down. There we find him and leave him, with customers in pearls and automobile veils, striving to catch his excellently graduated nod of recognition.

There is a large round table in the northeast corner of André's at which six can sit. To this table Grainger and Mary Adrian made their way. Kappelman and Reeves were already there. And Miss Tooker, who designed the May cover for the *Ladies' Notathome Magazine*. And Mrs. Pothunter, who never drank anything but black and white highballs, being in mourning for her husband, who — oh, I've forgotten what he did — died, like as not.

Spaghetti-weary reader, wouldst take one penny-in-the-slot peep into the fair land of Bohemia? Then look; and when you think you have seen it you have not. And it is neither thimbleriggery nor astigmatism.

The walls of the Café André were covered with original sketches by the artists who furnished much of the color and sound of the place. Fair woman furnished the theme for the bulk of the drawings. When you say " sirens and siphons " you come near to estimating the alliterative atmosphere of André's.

First, I want you to meet my friend, Miss Adrian. Miss Tooker and Mrs. Pothunter you already know. While she tucks in the fingers of her elbow gloves you shall have her daguerreotype. So faint and uncertain shall the portrait be:

Age, somewhere between twenty-seven and high-neck evening dresses. Camaraderie in large bunches — whatever the fearful word may mean. Habitat — anywhere from Seattle to Terra del Fuego. Temperament uncharted — she let Reeves squeeze her hand after he recited one of his poems; but she counted the change after sending him out with a dollar to buy some pickled pig's feet. Deportment 75 out of a possible 100. Morals 100.

Mary was one of the princesses of Bohemia. In the first place, it was a royal and a daring thing to have been named Mary. There are twenty Fifines and Heloises to one Mary in the Country of Elusion.

Now her gloves are tucked in. Miss Tooker has assumed a June poster pose; Mrs. Pothunter has bitten her lips to make the red show; Reeves has several times felt his coat to make sure that his latest poem is in the pocket. (It had been neatly typewritten; but he has copied it on the backs of letters with a pencil.) Kappelman is underhandedly watching the clock. It is ten minutes to nine. When the hour comes it is to remind him of a story. Synopsis: A French girl says to her suitor: "Did you ask my father for my hand at nine o'clock this morning, as you said you would?" "I did not," he replies. "At nine o'clock I was fighting a duel with swords in the Bois de Boulogne." "Coward!" she hisses.

The dinner was ordered. You know how the Bohemian feast of reason keeps up with the courses. Humor with the oysters; wit with the soup; repartee with the entrée; brag with the roast; knocks for Whistler and Kipling with the salad; songs with the coffee; the slapsticks with the cordials.

Between Miss Adrian's eyebrows was the pucker that shows the intense strain it requires to be at ease in Bohemia. Pat must come each sally, *mot*, and epigram. Every second of deliberation upon a reply costs you a bay leaf. Fine as a hair, a line began to curve from her nostril to her mouth. To hold her own not a chance must be missed. A sentence addressed to her must be as a piccolo, each word of it a stop, which she must be prepared to seize upon and play. And she must always be quicker than a Micmac Indian to paddle the light canoe of conversation away from the rocks in the rapids that flow from the Pierian spring. For, plodding reader, the handwriting on the wall in the banquet hall of Bohemia is " *Laisser faire.*" The gray ghost that sometimes peeps through the rings of smoke is that of slain old King Convention. Freedom is the tyrant that holds them in slavery.

As the dinner waned, hands reached for the pepper cruet rather than for the shaker of Attic salt. Miss

Tooker, with an elbow to business, leaned across the table toward Grainger, upsetting her glass of wine.

"Now while you are fed and in good humor," she said, "I want to make a suggestion to you about a new cover."

"A good idea," said Grainger, mopping the table-cloth with his napkin. "I'll speak to the waiter about it."

Kappelman, the painter, was the cut-up. As a piece of delicate Athenian wit he got up from his chair and waltzed down the room with a waiter. That dependent, no doubt an honest, pachydermatous, worthy, tax-paying, art-despising biped, released himself from the unequal encounter, carried his professional smile back to the dumb-waiter and dropped it down the shaft to eternal oblivion. Reeves began to make Keats turn in his grave. Mrs. Pothunter told the story of the man who met the widow on the train. Miss Adrian hummed what it still called a *chanson* in the cafés of Bridgeport. Grainger edited each individual effort with his assistant editor's smile, which meant: "Great! but you'll have to send them in through the regular channels. If I were the chief now — but you know how it is."

And soon the head waiter bowed before them, desolated to relate that the closing hour had already become chronologically historical; so out all trooped into the starry midnight, filling the street with gay laughter, to be barked at by hopeful cabmen and enviously eyed by the dull inhabitants of an uninspired world.

Grainger left Mary at the elevator in the trackless palm forest of the Idealia. After he had gone she came down again carrying a small hand-bag, 'phoned for a cab, drove to the Grand Central Station, boarded a 12.55 commuter's train, rode four hours with her burnt-umber head bobbing against the red-plush back of the seat, and landed during a fresh, stinging, glorious sunrise at a deserted station, the size of a peach crate, called Crocusville.

She walked a mile and clicked the latch of a gate. A bare, brown cottage stood twenty yards back; an old man with a pearl-white, Calvinistic face and clothes dyed blacker than a raven in a coal-mine was washing his hands in a tin basin on the front porch.

" How are you, father? " said Mary timidly.

" I am as well as Providence permits, Mary Ann. You will find your mother in the kitchen."

In the kitchen a cryptic, gray woman kissed her glacially on the forehead, and pointed out the potatoes which were not yet peeled for breakfast. Mary sat in a wooden chair and decorticated spuds, with a thrill in her heart.

For breakfast there were grace, cold bread, potatoes, bacon, and tea.

" You are pursuing the same avocation in the city

concerning which you have advised us from time to time by letter, I trust," said her father.

"Yes," said Mary, "I am still reviewing books for the same publication."

After breakfast she helped wash the dishes, and then all three sat in straight-back chairs in the bare-floored parlor.

"It is my custom," said the old man, "on the Sabbath day to read aloud from the great work entitled the 'Apology for Authorized and Set Forms of Liturgy,' by the ecclesiastical philosopher and revered theologian, Jeremy Taylor."

"I know it," said Mary blissfully, folding her hands.

For two hours the numbers of the great Jeremy rolled forth like the notes of an oratorio played on the violoncello. Mary sat gloating in the new sensation of racking physical discomfort that the wooden chair brought her. Perhaps there is no happiness in life so perfect as the martyr's. Jeremy's minor chords soothed her like the music of a tom-tom. "Why, oh why," she said to herself, "does some one not write words to it?"

At eleven they went to church in Crocusville. The back of the pine bench on which she sat had a penitential forward tilt that would have brought St. Simeon down, in jealousy, from his pillar. The preacher singled her out, and thundered upon her vicarious head the damnation of the world. At each side of her an adamant parent held her rigidly to the bar of judgment. An ant crawled upon her neck, but she dared not move. She lowered her eyes before the congregation — a hundred-eyed Cerberus that watched the gates through which her sins were fast thrusting her. Her soul was filled with a delirious, almost a fanatic joy. For she was out of the clutch of the tyrant, Freedom. Dogma and creed pinioned her with beneficent cruelty, as steel braces bind the feet of a crippled child. She was hedged, adjured, shackled, shored up, strait-jacketed, silenced, ordered. When they came out the minister stopped to greet them. Mary could only hang her head and answer " Yes, sir," and " No, sir," to his questions. When she saw that the other women carried their hymn-books at their waists with their left hands, she blushed and moved hers there, too, from her right.

She took the three-o'clock train back to the city. At nine she sat at the round table for dinner in the Café André. Nearly the same crowd was there.

" Where have you been to-day? " asked Mrs. Pothunter. " I 'phoned to you at twelve."

" I have been away in Bohemia," answered Mary, with a mystic smile.

There! Mary has given it away. She has spoiled my climax. For I was to have told you that Bohemia is nothing more than the little country in which you do not live. If you try to obtain citizenship in it, at once the court and retinue pack the royal archives and treasure and move away beyond the hills. It is a hillside that you turn your head to peer at from the windows of the Through Express.

At exactly half past eleven Kappelman, deceived by a new softness and slowness of *riposte* and parry in Mary Adrian, tried to kiss her. Instantly she slapped his face with such strength and cold fury that he shrank down, sobered, with the flaming red print of a hand across his leering features. And all sounds ceased, as when the shadows of great wings come upon a flock of chattering sparrows. One had broken the paramount law of sham-Bohemia — the law of " *Laisser faire*." The shock came not from the blow delivered, but from the blow received. With the effect of a schoolmaster entering the play-room of his pupils was that blow administered. Women pulled down their sleeves and laid prim hands against their ruffled side locks. Men looked at their watches. There was nothing of the effect of a brawl about it; it was purely the still panic produced by the sound of the ax of the fly cop, Conscience hammering at the gambling-house doors of the Heart.

With their punctilious putting on of cloaks, with their exaggerated pretense of not having seen or heard, with their stammering exchange of unaccustomed formalities, with their false show of a light-

[230]

THE COUNTRY OF ELUSION

hearted exit I must take leave of my Bohemian party.
Mary has robbed me of my climax; and she may go.

But I am not defeated. Somewhere there exists a
great vault miles broad and miles long — more ca-
pacious than the champagne caves of France. In
that vault are stored the anticlimaxes that should have
been tagged to all the stories that have been told in
the world. I shall cheat that vault of one deposit.

Minnie Brown, with her aunt, came from Crocusville down to the city to see the sights. And because
she had escorted me to fishless trout streams and ex-
hibited to me open-plumbed waterfalls and broken my
camera while I Julyed in her village, I must escort her
to the hives containing the synthetic clover honey of
town.

Especially did the custom-made Bohemia charm
her. The spaghetti wound its tendrils about her
heart; the free red wine drowned her belief in the
existence of commercialism in the world; she was dazed
and enchanted by the rugose wit that can be churned
out of California claret.

But one evening I got her away from the smell of
halibut and linoleum long enough to read to her the
manuscript of this story, which then ended before her
entrance into it. I read it to her because I knew that
all the printing-presses in the world were running to
try to please her and some others. And I asked her
about it.

"I didn't quite catch the trains," said she. "How long was Mary in Crocusville?"

"Ten hours and five minutes," I replied.

"Well, then, the story may do," said Minnie. "But if she had stayed there a week Kappelman would have got his kiss."

THE FERRY OF UNFULFILMENT

At the street corner, as solid as granite in the " rush-hour " tide of humanity, stood the Man from Nome. The Arctic winds and sun had stained him berry-brown. His eye still held the azure glint of the glaciers.

He was as alert as a fox, as tough as a caribou cutlet and as broad-gauged as the aurora borealis. He stood sprayed by a Niagara of sound — the crash of the elevated trains, clanging cars, pounding of rubberless tires and the antiphony of the cab and truck-drivers indulging in scarifying repartee. And so, with his gold dust cashed in to the merry air of a hundred thousand, and with the cakes and ale of one week in Gotham turning bitter on his tongue, the Man from Nome sighed to set foot again in Chilkoot, the exit from the land of street noises and Dead Sea apple pies.

Up Sixth avenue, with the tripping, scurrying, chattering bright-eyed, homing tide came the Girl from Sieber-Mason's. The Man from Nome looked and saw, first, that she was supremely beautiful after his own conception of beauty; and next, that she moved with exactly the steady grace of a dog sled on

[233]

a level crust of snow. His third sensation was an instantaneous conviction that he desired her greatly for his own. This quickly do men from Nome make up their minds. Besides, he was going back to the North in a short time, and to act quickly was no less necessary.

A thousand girls from the great department store of Sieber-Mason flowed along the sidewalk, making navigation dangerous to men whose feminine field of vision for three years has been chiefly limited to Siwash and Chilkat squaws. But the Man from Nome, loyal to her who had resurrected his long cached heart, plunged into the stream of pulchritude and followed her.

Down Twenty-third street she glided swiftly, looking to neither side; no more flirtatious than the bronze Diana above the Garden. Her fine brown hair was neatly braided; her neat waist and unwrinkled black skirt were eloquent of the double virtues — taste and economy. Ten yards behind followed the smitten Man from Nome.

Miss Claribel Colby, the Girl from Sieber-Mason's, belonged to that sad company of mariners known as Jersey commuters. She walked into the waiting-room of the ferry, and up the stairs, and by a marvellous swift, little run, caught the ferry-boat that was just going out. The Man from Nome closed up his ten yards in three jumps and gained the deck close beside her.

Miss Colby chose a rather lonely seat on the outside of the upper-cabin. The night was not cold, and she desired to be away from the curious eyes and tedious voices of the passengers. Besides, she was extremely weary and drooping from lack of sleep. On the previous night she had graced the annual ball and oyster fry of the West Side Wholesale Fish Dealers' Assistants' Social Club No. 2, thus reducing her usual time of sleep to only three hours.

And the day had been uncommonly troublous. Customers had been inordinately trying; the buyer in her department had scolded her roundly for letting her stock run down; her best friend, Mamie Tuthill, had snubbed her by going to lunch with that Dockery girl.

The Girl from Sieber-Mason's was in that relaxed, softened mood that often comes to the independent feminine wage-earner. It is a mood most propitious for the man who would woo her. Then she has yearnings to be set in some home and heart; to be comforted, and to hide behind some strong arm and rest, rest. But Miss Claribel Colby was also very sleepy.

There came to her side a strong man, browned and dressed carelessly in the best of clothes, with his hat in his hand.

" Lady," said the Man from Nome, respectfully, " excuse me for speaking to you, but I — I — I saw you on the street, and — and —"

" Oh, gee! " remarked the Girl from Sieber-Mason's, glancing up with the most capable coolness. " Ain't there any way to ever get rid of you mashers? I've tried everything from eating onions to using hat-pins. Be on your way, Freddie."

" I'm not one of that kind, lady," said the Man from Nome —" honest, I'm not. As I say, I saw you on the street, and I wanted to know you so bad I couldn't help followin' after you. I was afraid I wouldn't ever see you again in this big town unless I spoke; and that's why I done so."

Miss Colby looked once shrewdly at him in the dim light on the ferry-boat. No; he did not have the per-fidious smirk or the brazen swagger of the lady-killer. Sincerity and modesty shone through his boreal tan. It seemed to her that it might be good to hear a little of what he had to say.

" You may sit down," she said, laying her hand over a yawn with ostentatious politeness; "and — mind — don't get fresh or I'll call the steward."

The Man from Nome sat by her side. He admired her greatly. He more than admired her. She had exactly the looks he had tried so long in vain to find in a woman. Could she ever come to like him? Well, that was to be seen. He must do all in his power to stake his claim, anyhow.

"My name's Blayden," said he —"Henry Blayden."

"Are you real sure it ain't Jones?" asked the girl, leaning toward him, with delicious, knowing raillery.

"I'm down from Nome," he went on with anxious seriousness. "I scraped together a pretty good lot of dust up there, and brought it down with me."

"Oh, say!" she rippled, pursuing persiflage with engaging lightness, "then you must be on the White Wings force. I thought I'd seen you somewhere."

"You didn't see me on the street to-day when I saw you."

"I never look at fellows on the street."

"Well, I looked at you; and I never looked at anything before that I thought was half as pretty."

"Shall I keep the change?"

"Yes, I reckon so. I reckon you could keep anything I've got. I reckon I'm what you would call a rough man, but I could be awful good to anybody I liked. I've had a rough time of it up yonder, but I beat the game. Nearly 5,000 ounces of dust was what I cleaned up while I was there."

"Goodness!" exclaimed Miss Colby, obligingly sympathetic. "It must be an awful dirty place, wherever it is."

And then her eyes closed. The voice of the Man

from Nome had a monotony in its very earnestness. Besides, what dull talk was this of brooms and sweeping and dust? She leaned her head back against the wall.

"Miss," said the Man from Nome, with deeper earnestness and monotony, "I never saw anybody I liked as well as I do you. I know you can't think that way of me right yet; but can't you give me a chance? Won't you let me know you, and see if I can't make you like me?"

The head of the Girl from Sieber-Mason's slid over gently and rested upon his shoulder. Sweet sleep had won her, and she was dreaming rapturously of the Wholesale Fish Dealers' Assistants' ball.

The gentleman from Nome kept his arms to himself. He did not suspect sleep, and yet he was too wise to attribute the movement to surrender. He was greatly and blissfully thrilled, but he ended by regarding the head upon his shoulder as an encouraging preliminary, merely advanced as a harbinger of his success, and not to be taken advantage of.

One small speck of alloy discounted the gold of his satisfaction. Had he spoken too freely of his wealth? He wanted to be liked for himself.

"I want to say, Miss," he said, "that you can count on me. They know me in the Klondike from Juneau to Circle City and down the whole length of the Yukon. Many a night I've laid in the snow up there where I worked like a slave for three years, and wondered if I'd ever have anybody to like me. I didn't want all that dust just for myself. I thought I'd meet just the right one some time, and I done it to-day. Money's a mighty good thing to have, but to have the love of the one you like best is better still. If you was ever to marry a man, Miss, which would you rather he'd have? "

" Cash! "

The word came sharply and loudly from Miss Colby's lips, giving evidence that in her dreams she was now behind her counter in the great department store of Sieber-Mason.

Her head suddenly bobbed over sideways. She awoke, sat straight, and rubbed her eyes. The Man from Nome was gone.

" Gee! I believe I've been asleep," said Miss Colby. " Wonder what became of the White Wings! "

THE TALE OF A TAINTED TENNER

MONEY talks. But you may think that the conversation of a little old ten-dollar bill in New York would be nothing more than a whisper. Oh, very well! Pass up this *sotto voce* autobiography of an X if you like. If you are one of the kind that prefers to listen to John D.'s checkbook roar at you through a megaphone as it passes by, all right. But don't forget that small change can say a word to the point now and then. The next time you tip your grocer's clerk a silver quarter to give you extra weight of his boss's goods read the four words above the lady's head. How are they for repartee?

I am a ten-dollar Treasury note, series of 1901. You may have seen one in a friend's hand. On my face, in the centre, is a picture of the bison Americanus, miscalled a buffalo by fifty or sixty millions of Americans. The heads of Capt. Lewis and Capt. Clark adorn the ends. On my back is the graceful figure of Liberty or Ceres or Maxine Elliott standing in the centre of the stage on a conservatory plant. My references is — or are — Section 3,588, Revised Statutes. Ten cold, hard dollars — I don't say whether silver, gold, lead or iron — Uncle Sam will

THE TALE OF A TAINTED TENNER

hand you over his counter if you want to cash me in.

I beg you will excuse any conversational breaks that I make — thanks, I knew you would — got that sneaking little respect and agreeable feeling toward even an X, haven't you? You see, a tainted bill doesn't have much chance to acquire a correct form of expression. I never knew a really cultured and educated person that could afford to hold a ten-spot any longer than it would take to do an Arthur Duffy to the nearest That's All! sign or delicatessen store.

For a six-year-old, I've had a lively and gorgeous circulation. I guess I've paid as many debts as the man who dies. I've been owned by a good many kinds of people. But a little old ragged, damp, dingy five-dollar silver certificate gave me a jar one day. I was next to it in the fat and bad-smelling purse of a butcher.

"Hey, you Sitting Bull," says I, "don't scrouge so. Anyhow, don't you think it's about time you went in on a customs payment and got reissued? For a series of 1899 you're a sight."

"Oh, don't get crackly just because you're a Buffalo bill," says the fiver. "You'd be limp, too, if you'd been stuffed down in a thick cotton-and-lisle-thread under an elastic all day, and the thermometer not a degree under 85 in the store."

"I never heard of a pocketbook like that," says I. "Who carried you?"

" A shopgirl," says the five-spot.

" What's that? " I had to ask.

" You'll never know till their millennium comes,"
says the fiver.

Just then a two-dollar bill behind me with a George
Washington head, spoke up to the fiver:

" Aw, cut out yer kicks. Ain't lisle thread good
enough for yer? If you was under all cotton like
I've been to-day, and choked up with factory dust till
the lady with the cornucopia on me sneezed half a
dozen times, you'd have some reason to complain."

That was the next day after I arrived in New York.
I came in a $500 package of tens to a Brooklyn bank
from one of its Pennsylvania correspondents — and I
haven't made the acquaintance of any of the five and
two spot's friends' pocketbooks yet. Silk for mine,
every time.

I was lucky money. I kept on the move. Sometimes I changed hands twenty times a day. I saw
the inside of every business; I fought for my owner's
every pleasure. It seemed that on Saturday nights I
never missed being slapped down on a bar. Tens
were always slapped down, while ones and twos were
slid over to the bartenders folded. I got in the habit
of looking for mine, and I managed to soak in a little
straight or some spilled Martini or Manhattan when-
e er I could. Once I got tied up in a great greasy
r ll of bills in a pushcart peddler's jeans. I thought

THE TALE OF A TAINTED TENNER

I never would get in circulation again, for the future department store owner lived on eight cents' worth of dog meat and onions a day. But this peddler got into trouble one day on account of having his cart too near a crossing, and I was rescued. I always will feel grateful to the cop that got me. He changed me at a cigar store near the Bowery that was running a crap game in the back room. So it was the Captain of the precinct, after all, that did me the best turn, when he got his. He blew me for wine the next evening in a Broadway restaurant; and I really felt as glad to get back again as an Astor does when he sees the lights of Charing Cross.

A tainted ten certainly does get action on Broadway. I was alimony once, and got folded in a little dogskin purse among a lot of dimes. They were bragging about the busy times there were in Ossining whenever three girls got hold of one of them during the ice cream season. But it's Slow Moving Vehicles Keep to the Right for the little Bok tips when you think of the way we bison plasters refuse to stick to anything during the rush lobster hour.

The first I ever heard of tainted money was one night when a good thing with a Van to his name threw me over with some other bills to buy a stack of blues.

About midnight a big, easy-going man with a fat face like a monk's and the eye of a janitor with his wages raised took me and a lot of other notes and rolled us into what is termed a " wad " among the money tainters.

" Ticket me for five hundred," said he to the banker, " and look out for everything, Charlie. I'm going out for a stroll in the glen before the moonlight fades from the brow of the cliff. If anybody finds the roof in their way there's $60,000 wrapped in a comic supplement in the upper left-hand corner of the safe. Be bold; everywhere be bold, but be not bowled over. 'Night."

I found myself between two $20 gold certificates. One of 'em says to me:

" Well, old shorthorn, you're in luck to-night. You'll see something of life. Old Jack's going to make the Tenderloin look like a hamburg steak."

" Explain," says I. " I'm used to joints, but I don't care for filet mignon with the kind of sauce you serve."

" 'Xcuse me," said the twenty. " Old Jack is the proprietor of this gambling house. He's going on a whiz to-night because he offered $50,000 to a church and it refused to accept it because they said his money was tainted."

" What is a church? " I asked.

" Oh, I forgot," says the twenty, " that I was talking to a tenner. Of course you don't know. You're too much to put into the contribution basket, and not enough to buy anything at a bazaar. A church is —

a large building in which penwipers and tidies are sold at $20 each."

I don't care much about chinning with gold certificates. There's a streak of yellow in 'em. All is not gold that's quitters.

Old Jack certainly was a gilt-edged sport. When it came his time to loosen up he never referred the waiter to an actuary.

By and by it got around that he was smiting the rock in the wilderness; and all along Broadway things with cold noses and hot gullets fell in on our trail. The third Jungle Book was there waiting for somebody to put covers on it. Old Jack's money may have had a taint to it, but all the same he had orders for his Camembert piling up on him every minute. First his friends rallied round him; and then the fellows that his friends knew by sight; and then a few of his enemies buried the hatchet; and finally he was buying souvenirs for so many Neapolitan fisher maidens and butterfly octettes that the head waiters were 'phoning all over town for Julian Mitchell to please come around and get them into some kind of order.

At last we floated into an uptown café that I knew by heart. When the hod-carriers' union in jackets and aprons saw us coming the chief goal kicker called out: "Six — eleven — forty-two — nineteen — twelve " to his men, and they put on nose guards till it was clear whether we meant Port Arthur or

Portsmouth. But Old Jack wasn't working for the furniture and glass factories that night. He sat down quiet and sang " Ramble " in a half-hearted way. His feelings had been hurt, so the twenty told me, because his offer to the church had been refused.

But the wassail went on; and Brady himself couldn't have hammered the thirst mob into a better imitation of the real penchant for the stuff that you screw out of a bottle with a napkin.

Old Jack paid the twenty above me for a round, leaving me on the outside of his roll. He laid the roll on the table and sent for the proprietor.

" Mike," says he, " here's money that the good people have refused. Will it buy of your wares in the name of the devil? They say it's tainted."

" I will," says Mike, " and I'll put it in the drawer next to the bills that was paid to the parson's daughter for kisses at the church fair to build a new parsonage for the parson's daughter to live in."

At 1 o'clock when the hod-carriers were making ready to close up the front and keep the inside open, a woman slips in the door of the restaurant and comes up to Old Jack's table. You've seen the kind — black shawl, creepy hair, ragged skirt, white face, eyes a cross between Gabriel's and a sick kitten's — the kind of woman that's always on the lookout for an automobile or the mendicancy squad — and she stands there without a word and looks at the money.

THE TALE OF A TAINTED TENNER

Old Jack gets up, peels me off the roll and hands me to her with a bow.

"Madam," says he, just like actors I've heard, "here is a tainted bill. I am a gambler. This bill came to me to-night from a gentleman's son. Where he got it I do not know. If you will do me the favor to accept it, it is yours."

The woman took me with a trembling hand.

"Sir," said she, "I counted thousands of this issue of bills into packages when they were virgin from the presses. I was a clerk in the Treasury Department. There was an official to whom I owed my position. You say they are tainted now. If you only knew — but I won't say any more. Thank you with all my heart, sir — thank you — thank you."

Where do you suppose that woman carried me almost at a run? To a bakery. Away from Old Jack and a sizzling good time to a bakery. And I get changed, and she does a Sheridan-twenty-miles-away with a dozen rolls and a section of jelly cake as big as a turbine water-wheel. Of course I lost sight of her then, for I was snowed up in the bakery, wondering whether I'd get changed at the drug store the next day in an alum deal or paid over to the cement works.

A week afterward I butted up against one of the one-dollar bills the baker had given the woman for change.

"Hallo, E35039669," says I, "weren't you in the change for me in a bakery last Saturday night?"

"Yep," says the solitaire in his free and easy style.

"How did the deal turn out?" I asked.

"She blew E17051431 for milk and round steak," says the one-spot. "She kept me till the rent man came. It was a bum room with a sick kid in it. But you ought to have seen him go for the bread and tincture of formaldehyde. Half-starved, I guess. Then she prayed some. Don't get stuck up, tenner. We one-spots hear ten prayers, where you hear one. She said something about ' who giveth to the poor.' Oh, let's cut out the slum talk. I'm certainly tired of the company that keeps me. I wish I was big enough to move in society with you tainted bills."

"Shut up," says I; "there's no such thing. I know the rest of it. There's a ' lendeth to the Lord' somewhere in it. Now look on my back and read what you see there."

"This note is a legal tender at its face value for all debts public and private."

"This talk about tainted money makes me tired," says I.

ELSIE IN NEW YORK

No, bumptious reader, this story is not a continuation of the Elsie series. But if your Elsie had lived over here in our big city there might have been a chapter in her books not very different from this.

Especially for the vagrant feet of youth are the roads of Manhattan beset " with pitfall and with gin." But the civic guardians of the young have made themselves acquainted with the snares of the wicked, and most of the dangerous paths are patrolled by their agents, who seek to turn straying ones away from the peril that menaces them. And this will tell you how they guided my Elsie safely through all peril to the goal that she was seeking.

Elsie's father had been a cutter for Fox & Otter, cloaks and furs, on lower Broadway. He was an old man, with a slow and limping gait, so a pot-hunter of a newly licensed chauffeur ran him down one day when livelier game was scarce. They took the old man home, where he lay on his bed for a year and then died, leaving $2.50 in cash and a letter from Mr. Otter offering to do anything he could to help his faithful old employee. The old cutter regarded this letter as a valuable legacy to his daughter, and he put it into her hands with pride as the shears of the dread Cleaner and Repairer snipped off his thread of life.

That was the landlord's cue; and forth he came and did his part in the great eviction scene. There was no snowstorm ready for Elsie to steal out into, drawing her little red woollen shawl about her shoulders, but she went out, regardless of the unities. And as for the red shawl — back to Blaney with it! Elsie's fall tan coat was cheap, but it had the style and fit of the best at Fox & Otter's. And her lucky stars had given her good looks, and eyes as blue and innocent as the new shade of note paper, and she had $1 left of the $2.50. And the letter from Mr. Otter. Keep your eye on the letter from Mr. Otter. That is the clue. I desire that everything be made plain as we go. Detective stories are so plentiful now that they do not sell.

And so we find Elsie, thus equipped, starting out in the world to seek her fortune. One trouble about the letter from Mr. Otter was that it did not bear the new address of the firm, which had moved about a month before. But Elsie thought she could find it. She had heard that policemen, when politely addressed, or thumbscrewed by an investigation committee, will give up information and addresses. So she boarded a downtown car at One Hundred and Seventy-seventh street and rode south to Forty-second, which she thought must surely be the end of the island. There she stood against the wall undecided, for the city's roar and dash was new to her. Up where she had lived was rural New York, so far out that the milkmen awaken you in the morning by the squeaking of pumps instead of the rattling of cans.

A kind-faced, sunburned young man in a soft-brimmed hat went past Elsie into the Grand Central Depot. That was Hank Ross, of the Sunflower Ranch, in Idaho, on his way home from a visit to the East. Hank's heart was heavy, for the Sunflower Ranch was a lonesome place, lacking the presence of a woman. He had hoped to find one during his visit who would congenially share his prosperity and home, but the girls of Gotham had not pleased his fancy. But, as he passed in, he noted, with a jumping of his pulses, the sweet, ingenuous face of Elsie and her pose of doubt and loneliness. With true and honest Western impulse he said to himself that here was his mate. He could love her, he knew; and he would surround her with so much comfort, and cherish her so carefully that she would be happy, and make two sunflowers grow on the ranch where there grew but one before.

Hank turned and went back to her. Backed by his never before questioned honesty of purpose, he approached the girl and removed his soft-brimmed hat. Elsie had but time to sum up his handsome frank face with one shy look of modest admiration when a burly cop hurled himself upon the ranchman, seized him by the collar and backed him against the wall. Two blocks away a burglar was coming out of an apartment-house with a bag of silverware on his shoulder; but that is neither here nor there.

" Carry on yez mashin' tricks right before me eyes, will yez? " shouted the cop. " I'll teach yez to speak to ladies on me beat that ye're not acquainted with. Come along."

Elsie turned away with a sigh as the ranchman was dragged away. She had liked the effect of his light blue eyes against his tanned complexion. She walked southward, thinking herself already in the district where her father used to work, and hoping to find some one who could direct her to the firm of Fox & Otter.

But did she want to find Mr. Otter? She had inherited much of the old cutter's independence. How much better it would be if she could find work and support herself without calling on him for aid!

Elsie saw a sign " Employment Agency " and went in. Many girls were sitting against the wall in chairs. Several well-dressed ladies were looking them over. One white-haired, kind-faced old lady in rustling black silk hurried up to Elsie.

" My dear," she said in a sweet, gentle voice, " are you looking for a position? I like your face and ap-

pearance so much. I want a young woman who will
be half maid and half companion to me. You will
have a good home and I will pay you $30 a month."

Before Elsie could stammer forth her gratified acceptance, a young woman with gold glasses on her
bony nose and her hands in her jacket pockets seized
her arm and drew her aside.

" I am Miss Ticklebaum," said she, " of the Association for the Prevention of Jobs Being Put Up on
Working Girls Looking for Jobs. We prevented
forty-seven girls from securing positions last week.
I am here to protect you. Beware of any one who
offers you a job. How do you know that this woman
does not want to make you work as a breaker-boy in
a coal mine or murder you to get your teeth? If
you accept work of any kind without permission of
our association you will be arrested by one of our
agents."

" But what am I to do? " asked Elsie. " I have no
home or money. I must do something. Why am I
not allowed to accept this kind lady's offer? "

" I do not know," said Miss Ticklebaum. " That
is the affair of our Committee on the Abolishment of
Employers. It is my duty simply to see that you do
not get work. You will give me your name and address and report to our secretary every Thursday.
We have 600 girls on the waiting list who will in time
be allowed to accept positions as vacancies occur on

our roll of Qualified Employers, which now comprises twenty-seven names. There is prayer, music and lemonade in our chapel the third Sunday of every month."

Elsie hurried away after thanking Miss Ticklebaum for her timely warning and advice. After all, it seemed that she must try to find Mr. Otter.

But after walking a few blocks she saw a sign, " Cashier wanted," in the window of a confectionery store. In she went and applied for the place, after casting a quick glance over her shoulder to assure herself that the job-preventer was not on her trail.

The proprietor of the confectionery was a benevo-lent old man with a peppermint flavor, who decided, after questioning Elsie pretty closely, that she was the very girl he wanted. Her services were needed at once, so Elsie, with a thankful heart, drew off her tan coat and prepared to mount the cashier's stool.

But before she could do so a gaunt lady wearing steel spectacles and black mittens stood before her, with a long finger pointing, and exclaimed: " Young woman, hesitate! "

Elsie hesitated.

" Do you know," said the black-and-steel lady, " that in accepting this position you may this day cause the loss of a hundred lives in agonizing physical torture and the sending as many souls to perdition? "

[254]

"Why, no," said Elsie, in frightened tones. "How could I do that?"

"Rum," said the lady —"the demon rum. Do you know why so many lives are lost when a theatre catches fire? Brandy balls. The demon rum lurking in brandy balls. Our society women while in theatres sit grossly intoxicated from eating these candies filled with brandy. When the fire fiend sweeps down upon them they are unable to escape. The candy stores are the devil's distilleries. If you assist in the distribution of these insidious confections you assist in the destruction of the bodies and souls of your fellow-beings, and in the filling of our jails, asylums and almshouses. Think, girl, ere you touch the money for which brandy balls are sold.

"Dear me," said Elsie, bewildered. "I didn't know there was rum in brandy balls. But I must live by some means. What shall I do?"

"Decline the position," said the lady, "and come with me. I will tell you what to do."

After Elsie had told the confectioner that she had changed her mind about the cashiership she put on her coat and followed the lady to the sidewalk, where awaited an elegant victoria.

"Seek some other work," said the black-and-steel lady, "and assist in crushing the hydra-headed demon rum." And she got into the victoria and drove away.

"I guess that puts it up to Mr. Otter again," said Elsie, ruefully, turning down the street. "And I'm sorry, too, for I'd much rather make my way without help."

Near Fourteenth street Elsie saw a placard tacked on the side of a doorway that read: "Fifty girls, neat sewers, wanted immediately on theatrical costumes. Good pay."

She was about to enter, when a solemn man, dressed all in black, laid his hand on her arm.

"My dear girl," he said, "I entreat you not to enter that dressing-room of the devil."

"Goodness me!" exclaimed Elsie, with some impatience. "The devil seems to have a cinch on all the business in New York. What's wrong about the place?"

"It is here," said the solemn man, "that the regalia of Satan — in other words, the costumes worn on the stage — are manufactured. The stage is the road to ruin and destruction. Would you imperil your soul by lending the work of your hands to its support? Do you know, my dear girl, what the theatre leads to? Do you know where actors and actresses go after the curtain of the playhouse has fallen upon them for the last time?"

"Sure," said Elsie. "Into vaudeville. But do you think it would be wicked for me to make a little money to live on by sewing? I must get something to do pretty soon."

"The flesh-pots of Egypt," exclaimed the reverend gentleman, uplifting his hands. "I beseech you, my child, to turn away from this place of sin and iniquity."

"But what will I do for a living?" asked Elsie. "I don't care to sew for this musical comedy, if it's as rank as you say it is; but I've got to have a job."

"The Lord will provide," said the solemn man. "There is a free Bible class every Sunday afternoon in the basement of the cigar store next to the church. Peace be with you. Amen. Farewell."

Elsie went on her way. She was soon in the downtown district where factories abound. On a large brick building was a gilt sign, "Posey & Trimmer, Artificial Flowers." Below it was hung a newly stretched canvas bearing the words, "Five hundred girls wanted to learn trade. Good wages from the start. Apply one flight up."

Elsie started toward the door, near which were gathered in groups some twenty or thirty girls. One big girl with a black straw hat tipped down over her eyes stepped in front of her.

"Say, you'se," said the girl, "are you'se goin' in there after a job?"

"Yes," said Elsie; "I must have work."

"Now don't do it," said the girl. "I'm chairman

of our Scab Committee. There's 400 of us girls locked out just because we demanded 50 cents a week raise in wages, and ice water, and for the foreman to shave off his mustache. You're too nice a looking girl to be a scab. Wouldn't you please help us along by trying to find a job somewhere else, or would you'se rather have your face pushed in? "

" I'll try somewhere else," said Elsie.

She walked aimlessly eastward on Broadway, and there her heart leaped to see the sign, " Fox & Otter," stretching entirely across the front of a tall building. It was as though an unseen guide had led her to it through the by-ways of her fruitless search for work.

She hurried into the store and sent in to Mr. Otter by a clerk her name and the letter he had written her father. She was shown directly into his private office.

Mr. Otter arose from his desk as Elsie entered and took both hands with a hearty smile of welcome. He was a slightly corpulent man of nearly middle age, a little bald, gold spectacled, polite, well dressed, radiating.

" Well, well, and so this is Beatty's little daughter! Your father was one of our most efficient and valued employees. He left nothing? Well, well. I hope we have not forgotten his faithful services. I am sure there is a vacancy now among our models. Oh, it is easy work — nothing easier."

Mr. Otter struck a bell. A long-nosed clerk thrust a portion of himself inside the door.

" Send Miss Hawkins in," said Mr. Otter. Miss Hawkins came.

" Miss Hawkins," said Mr. Otter, " bring for Miss Beatty to try on one of those Russian sable coats and — let's see — one of those latest model black tulle hats with white tips."

Elsie stood before the full-length mirror with pink cheeks and quick breath. Her eyes shone like faint stars. She was beautiful. Alas! she was beautiful.

I wish I could stop this story here. Confound it! I will. No; it's got to run it out. I didn't make it up. I'm just repeating it.

I'd like to throw bouquets at the wise cop, and the lady who rescues Girls from Jobs, and the prohibitionist who is trying to crush brandy balls, and the sky pilot who objects to costumes for stage people (there are others), and all the thousands of good people who are at work protecting young people from the pitfalls of a great city; and then wind up by pointing out how they were the means of Elsie reaching her father's benefactor and her kind friend and rescuer from poverty. This would make a fine Elsie story of the old sort. I'd like to do this; but there's just a word or two to follow.

While Elsie was admiring herself in the mirror, Mr.

Otter went to the telephone booth and called up some number. Don't ask me what it was.

"Oscar," said he, "I want you to reserve the same table for me this evening. . . . What? Why, the one in the Moorish room to the left of the shrubbery. . . . Yes; two. . . . Yes, the usual brand; and the '85 Johannisburger with the roast. If it isn't the right temperature I'll break your neck. . . . No; not her . . . No, indeed . . . A new one — a peacherino, Oscar, a peacherino!"

Tired and tiresome reader, I will conclude, if you please, with a paraphrase of a few words that you will remember were written by him — by him of Gad's Hill, before whom, if you doff not your hat, you shall stand with a covered pumpkin — aye, sir, a pumpkin.

Lost, Your Excellency. Lost, Associations and Societies. Lost, Right Reverends and Wrong Reverends of every order. Lost, Reformers and Lawmakers, born with heavenly compassion in your hearts, but with the reverence of money in your souls. And lost thus around us every day.

THE END.

THE COUNTRY LIFE PRESS
GARDEN CITY, N. Y.